The
Unlikely
Lawman

The Hewey Calloway Novels

By Elmer Kelton
The Smiling Country
The Good Old Boys
Six Bits a Day

By Steve Kelton
The Unlikely Lawman

ELMER KELTON'S

The Unlikely Lawman

A Hewey Calloway Adventure

BY STEVE KELTON

FORGE®

A TOM DOHERTY ASSOCIATES BOOK
NEW YORK

This is a work of fiction. All of the characters, organizations, and events portrayed in this novel are either products of the author's imagination or are used fictitiously.

ELMER KELTON'S THE UNLIKELY LAWMAN

Copyright © 2022 by Steve Kelton

All rights reserved.

Edited by Robert Davis

A Forge Book
Published by Tom Doherty Associates
120 Broadway
New York, NY 10271

www.tor-forge.com

Forge® is a registered trademark of Macmillan Publishing Group, LLC.

ISBN 978-1-250-83069-2

Our books may be purchased in bulk for promotional, educational, or business use. Please contact your local bookseller or the Macmillan Corporate and Premium Sales Department at 1–800-221-7945, extension 5442, or by email at MacmillanSpecialMarkets@macmillan.com.

First Edition: August 2022

Printed in the United States of America

0 9 8 7 6 5 4 3 2 1

The Unlikely Lawman

CHAPTER ONE

Hewey Calloway was in his element.

It was spring, and West Texas had on her Sunday best. The morning sun was warm, the effects of earlier rains beginning to show. Green shoots had appeared in the few clumps where grass grew, and much of the rest of the ground boasted tallow weed and other plants Hewey knew but couldn't name. Most of the cows he saw had babies by their sides, full udders, and a thin layer of fat beginning to show on their ribs and over their hip bones. The cows without calves were pig fat and would soon be cut off and sold as freeloaders that wouldn't earn their keep this year.

Hewey was on horseback, taking it all in with the pride of ownership, but without the headaches or expectation of reward. These were Two Cs cattle and belonged not to Hewey but to ranchman C. C. Tarpley, who had just fired Hewey at the chuck-wagon that morning.

It wasn't the first time Tarpley had fired Hewey, and it probably wouldn't be the last. Hewey had even quit once or twice himself, but the two always came to an accommodation eventually; Hewey was a good cowboy, and C.C. valued that, even if he didn't value it enough to pay well. Parsimony was a common condition among the ranch owners Hewey had known, though C. C. Tarpley displayed a more severe case than most.

Hewey had a month's worth of C.C.'s stingy pay in his pocket, a brown horse that would watch a cow, and he was gloriously unemployed.

So close to his fortieth birthday that he could hear it taunting him in quiet moments, Hewey was the older of two sons. Their widowed father had a restless streak that he stamped indelibly on his first-born. The three Calloways—Pa, Hewey, and brother Walter—had drifted constantly within the East Texas region of blackland farms, picking up what work was available to them. As a boy, Hewey drug a cotton sack for miles before he was big enough to put behind a mule and a pair of plow handles. They were an ill fit for his hands from the beginning, and Hewey chafed to be somewhere else, doing something else. Brother Walter, a year younger, took to farm work like he was born for it. It was only at Hewey's insistence after Pa died that the two brothers went west looking for cowboy jobs that were said to be plentiful in the Pecos River country, and the brothers found the job situation to be as advertised.

A decade and a half later, in 1904, Hewey had earned a reputation in West Texas and eastern New Mexico as a top hand, and Walter was back behind a plow, but this time it was his own, and he was turning back native sod on his own land. Walter was the only one of the Calloway clan, what little Hewey knew of it, to own land. Back in East Texas, where it rained, Walter's homestead would sound like an empire up against the farms that were common. In a moment of clarity, someone in the Texas legislature had realized years earlier that it didn't rain much west of San Angelo, and not a lot even there. The state had a world of West Texas land it couldn't use and was leasing it to cattlemen at a pittance for grazing. From then on, Texas law allowed homesteaders to claim up to four sections—four square miles—a full sixteen times as much as the average 160-acre farm back east.

It appeared generous to people in rainier regions, but it wouldn't run enough cows to sustain a single man, much less a man with a family. Walter was one of many West Texans who had a four-section outfit and a family, and most years the money ran out before the year did. His bride refused to give up, however, and at her insistence Walter began breaking out land to farm, first a few acres, then a few more.

The delta cotton of the Blacklands could never be grown here, so Walter planted feed crops instead. Hewey had counseled against the entire endeavor, reasoning that land that resented the cow would look even less kindly at the plow. That only got him cold stares from his sister-in-law.

Alvin Lawdermilk had his hands full supervising a small crew of cowboys sacking out young horses in the breaking pen, but he didn't miss the approaching rider.

"Howdy, Hewey," he said with a slight wave of his hand as Hewey dismounted, a friendly acknowledgment but not a broad enough movement to spook the excitable horses. He extended the hand to Hewey through the fence, then quietly eased out the gate and led the way to a spot on the shady side of the saddle barn.

Alvin was middle-aged and graying, a thin man with a slight stoop, but he was still strong enough to fight a recalcitrant horse or mule, his primary products. He left most of the bronc riding to younger hands, having hit the hard, dry ground more often than he cared to already. Besides, he no longer bounced like he had when he was younger.

"What are you doin' out footloose in the middle of a workday?" he asked Hewey. "Did ol' C.C. have a stroke and give you hands a vacation?"

"Just one of us. He gave me a permanent day off." Hewey gave a broad, slightly crooked grin.

"You two can't get along with or without each other. What'd you pull this time?"

"Wasn't much, but C.C. is pretty excitable and damned unreasonable sometimes. I was toppin' off one of the broncs in my string this mornin', just gettin' his kinks worked out so he'd settle down for the day's drive. The next thing I knew, we was right in the middle of camp, scatterin' cowboys left and right. I was doin' good to keep a leg on either side of him, and reinin' that renegade was out of the question, so you can see it wasn't my fault.

"Even at that the whole thing would've made for a good laugh if ol' C.C. hadn't been right square in that bronc's sights. I gotta admit, for a short, stove-up old man, C.C. can still move pretty good when he's about to git ground into the dirt. By the time the dust cleared he was cussin' me and I was cussin' his miserly taste in horseflesh. He blowed up and said his horses was just fine, but if I didn't like 'em I could draw my time and go ride somebody else's horses.

"So here I am, ridin' my own."

"If you'd got yourself fired a week earlier, I'd have let a couple of these knuckleheads ride on past. They don't have any trouble bellyin' up to the table, and they can find their bedrolls just fine, but you've gotta lead 'em by the hand to everything else."

"Thanks all the same, Alvin," Hewey said, "but I ain't looking for work just yet. I've got a month's pay to carry me a while, and I ain't been fired long enough to enjoy it."

"Does Eve know?" Alvin's tone took on a note of gravity as he asked.

"I haven't been by Walter and Eve's place yet. Your outfit is closer to where the wagon was when me and C.C. had our disagreement."

"Well, then you'll stay the night. You missed dinner, but supper will be ready in a few hours."

"I'd sure like to, Alvin, but I reckon I oughta water out and get on over to Walter's and see which way the wind's blowin'."

"I can tell you right now it'll be blowin' straight into your face."

"Oh, Eve ain't always on a tear, Alvin. I've caught my sister-in-law in a good mood two, maybe three times."

"And how long did that last?"

"Not very long with me around," Hewey acknowledged, wincing at the memory. He thought that Alvin's mother-in-law was just as disapproving. Alvin didn't need to be reminded of that, however, so Hewey didn't.

"I'll sure miss havin' the company of your womenfolk at a civilized table, Alvin, but if you'll give 'em my regards, I'd best get on."

"You're a damned poor liar, Hewey Calloway," Alvin said with a chuckle. "You won't miss Mother Faversham any more than I would if she wandered off in the dark one night and never come home. But two doses of that medicine in the same day are too many for any man, and I have a hunch you'll get a big dose from Eve."

Old Lady Faversham, as she was known behind her back to the Lawdermilk crew and most any cowboy who'd ever joined it for a spell, was a grumpy, bitter old woman for reasons Hewey couldn't fathom. Someone had done her wrong at some point in her life, or at least she thought so, but it was long before Hewey met her. He just knew that she focused most of her ire against any man who came within range. She was strong in her opinions and not at all modest about sharing them.

They shook hands again, and Hewey remounted for the short ride to the water trough. Like most cowboys, it would never dawn on him to walk and lead his mount; horses were for riding.

"I'm gettin' old, Hewey; I almost forgot. I'll have a job for you in a couple or three weeks, assuming my good hands and those two knuckleheads have these fillies shaped up by then. A fellow near Durango, Colorado, has contracted for the lot, more than seventy head. If you're available, I'd like you to take 'em."

"Don't they raise horses in Colorado?"

"They raise a lot, but not like mine," Alvin answered with pride. "There's something about the Pecos River."

Hewey knew the difference was in the horse savvy, and Alvin had that.

"Sorry about you gettin' fired, Hewey, but it was a stroke of luck for me. You're just the man for this little job. I've never seen anybody take to the cowboy life like you."

"Appreciate the offer, Alvin. I've never seen that country. I'll think on it."

Hewey was glad he'd made the slight detour to the Lawdermilk place. If he'd hit Walter's an hour earlier, he would have come face-to-face with Eve Calloway, alone. As it was, Walter had just finished watering the wagon team and was between the rough barn and the equally spare house when Hewey rode up.

The Calloway homestead wasn't much to look at. Even Hewey was of that opinion, and he'd helped Walter build it all. The house was what was referred to as box-and-strip construction. Set up on stacks of flat rocks, the structure was built of wide, rough-cut boards nailed vertically, the gaps between them covered by narrower strips. The roof was rude wood shingles that shrank in the dry air until sunlight filtered through in the daytime, and a full moon provided enough interior lighting to see by. The shingles quickly swelled when challenged by the occasional rainstorm, however, and the interior remained mostly dry.

Wind whistled through the walls at first, but Eve gradually stopped that with old newspapers and flour paste, light on the precious flour. With opportunities for schooling scarce, Eve made double duty of the newspapered walls by teaching both boys to read, mostly with headlines that celebrated the advances of the closing century and speculated wildly about miracles to come in the new one. Nothing stopped the wind that came up through the plank floor except rugs, and those were limited, as were other amenities.

The Calloways' barn was of similar construction, minus the wallpaper and rugs. Neither house nor barn had seen any paint, inside or out, for paint cost money. The corrals were not a square foot larger than necessary, and a windmill and cypress storage tank with a rock and concrete water trough completed the layout. Eve's chickens roosted under the lean-to shed attached to the barn, and she made a daily round of brush clumps to collect the hidden eggs before a raccoon, skunk, or ringtail found them first.

The Calloways lived little if any better than sharecroppers back east, with but one exception: they had lived there long enough to satisfy the Homestead law, and they had a deed from the State of Texas to prove that the land was theirs. To Walter and Eve that meant the world.

To Hewey it looked more like a life sentence of hard labor.

"Well, if it ain't the Prodigal Brother!" Walter exclaimed when he saw Hewey. "What in the world brings you by here on Two Cs business?"

"I ain't with the Tarpley outfit anymore; I'm here on my own business," Hewey answered with a broad grin.

Walter's own smile faded just a bit when he heard that, and Hewey noticed.

"Reckon I'll see to Biscuit, while you break the news to Eve."

"Break what news to me?" Eve had seen the rider and walked up on them while neither was looking.

"Now, Eve, I've got somethin' lined up . . ." Hewey began.

"Speak English, Hewey Calloway."

"I been fired, Eve."

Eve laughed, and the two men cut a glance at each other. "I was afraid you'd fooled around and married some floozie. You've been fired before. The two of you wash up and come to the house. I baked a pie earlier, and there should be just enough to go around. We'll celebrate your visit."

With that, Eve turned toward the house, leaving two dumbfounded men staring in her wake.

"Walter," Hewey said solemnly, "some fool's gone and kidnapped your wife."

Little Tommy was the first of Hewey's two nephews to spot him, and came running, kicking up puffs of dust with his bare feet.

"Uncle Hewey!" he yelled, wrapping his arms around Hewey at waist level, almost knocking him off balance. His older brother, Cotton, was absorbed with something in the wagon bed and had yet to look up. In his middle teens, Cotton had grown proficient with a rope and could handle a horse as well as most grown men, but had a fascination with tools and the machines they were designed to manipulate.

As they approached the wagon, Tommy said, "Look what we brought Mama! Ain't it nice?"

Hewey could see some sort of bucket contraption with metal pieces attached. It was too big to be a mop pail and too small to be a water trough. Hewey was at a loss.

"Why, that sure is . . . somethin'," he said.

Cotton pulled his attention away from the device and explained, "It's a clothes washing machine, Uncle Hewey. You put water in it, turn this crank, and it cleans clothes."

"Where's the rub board?" Hewey asked, still confused and a little uncertain his nephew knew what he was tinkering with.

"These paddles in here rub the clothes together. Saves all that work."

Hewey thought turning the crank looked like a lot of work in itself.

"Mainly it will save time, and that will let me get more done in a day."

That was Eve, who had walked up on them unobserved again. Her ability to do that always spooked Hewey a little.

Hewey began to understand Eve's unaccustomed good mood; if there was anything that pleased his sister-in-law, it was getting more done in a day. He noticed long ago that she had extended her expectations of productivity to Walter, and later to the boys. Walter was younger than Hewey, but between work and worry, he was beginning to look like the elder of the two. His hair was thinning and his face carried deeper lines, partly from the blazing West Texas sun, and partly from mental stress. Hewey, by contrast, seldom worried about anything, and he took a casual approach to work as well. He labored constantly on horseback, but didn't count that as work.

"I figured out what's wrong with this washer, Mama," Cotton said. "This bracket here has stretched, and the gears won't mesh. I'll have it good as new in no time."

Hewey marveled at his nephew's ability with machinery, a gift he himself didn't have and didn't want; let it get around in this modern age that you could fix mechanical things, and you might as well put your saddle away. He thought it a shame, though, that Cotton's talent might cost the country a good cowboy in the making, especially since Walter now found himself shackled to the plow. It was Hewey's fervent hope that little Tommy wouldn't also be led astray from the righteous path.

"What does a thing like that cost?" Hewey asked, and immediately regretted the question; if there was anything that Eve valued as highly as work, it was a dollar, a commodity that was always in short supply wherever the Calloways happened to be.

"It didn't cost us nothin' except a little work," Tommy answered quickly, evidently eager to relay the news to Hewey before his older brother could. "The Johnsons went broke and sold out to Mr. Tarpley. We helped 'em load their stuff this mornin', and they gave us the clothes washer. Mrs. Johnson hated to part with it, but she said there wasn't room in the wagon for somethin' that didn't work. And Mr. Johnson gave me a pocketknife."

Tommy fished a rusted relic out of his pocket and showed it to Hewey proudly. The lone blade had a broken tip, and the grips were gone. Still, it was a rare treasure to his nephew.

"I reckon you'll turn into a first-class whittler with that," Hewey said admiringly.

"First thing I'm gonna whittle is some new sides," Tommy said. "Them brads stickin' out sure bite into a man's hand."

Hewey figured they bit into a boy's hand a lot worse.

Hewey savored his generous slice of pie and was the last to finish. Walter and the boys had left to deal with the afternoon's chores when he carried his plate to Eve's steaming dishpan.

"I was about half serious when I said that about the floozies." Eve's back was turned, but her words were directed at him.

"Aw, Eve, I don't even know any floozies."

"Hewey Calloway!" Eve turned around then and, planting her wet hands on her hips, gave him the same arched eyebrow she would give a little boy who denied taking cookies with his hand still in the jar.

"Well, not by name, anyway," Hewey said by way of explanation.

"Hewey, you're a nice-looking man, and when you flash that big, crooked grin of yours, women notice. They like you, Hewey; they can't help it." She paused briefly and sighed again, eyeing him in a way that made Hewey a bit uncomfortable. It wasn't her usual glare, but a soft look he'd seen a few women give to men who had caught their eyes.

Eve was what Hewey considered a handsome woman. She couldn't be called beautiful, but Hewey was sure she had been pretty in her younger years. The fashion of the time ran to considerably more flesh than Eve carried on her moderate frame, but Hewey had to concede that all the Calloways spent a lot more time working than eating, and Eve was no more spare than Walter or Hewey himself. Eve also spent almost as much time in the sun as Walter and worried no less, so the lines in her face were all well earned, and she had neither the time, the potions, nor the vanity to try to hide them. Still, there was something attractive about her, at least when she didn't have her back up over something.

"I just want you to pick the right woman, one who will make you a home and give you a family."

"I'm a cowboy, Eve, and a purty good one if it ain't immodest of me to say so. I don't know anything else, and I'm happy to be what I know how to be."

"All I'm saying is that life is short, and a man who doesn't settle down by the time he's your age . . ." Eve left it at that, and Hewey felt lucky to escape the house without any further discussion.

The next few days went quickly. It took Hewey and Walter only half a day to gather the handful of calves, brand and earmark them all, and turn the little bulls into little steers. By bringing the boys into the job, however, Hewey had stretched a half-day's work into most of a day. It was good to see Walter horseback again, flipping a rope instead of plow reins. Hewey even missed a few loops deliberately to give his brother a chance.

It had been a good day, but it came at a price.

When the four of them rode in, laughing and joking, they found a sullen Eve.

"I thought you and Cotton were going to break out some more land this afternoon," she said coldly to Walter. "The day's almost gone, and the team hasn't left the corral."

"We'll get to that first thing in the morning," Walter answered, and Hewey noticed that his shoulders suddenly sagged.

"And still be half a day behind," Eve said sharply, turning on her heel and striding stiffly toward the house. All night long, Hewey half expected Walter to show up at the saddle shed, toting a blanket.

Walter put in long hours on the plow the next day—and the next. Cotton was right at his side. Before long, they had made up the lost half day and even gotten a little ahead of Eve's ambitious schedule. For his part, Hewey took Tommy to cut mesquite fence posts and gather firewood in a brushy draw.

Eve's mood gradually lightened as Walter and Cotton's freshly turned soil stretched farther and farther. The day came when Hewey felt relaxed enough to make a real mistake.

Wild game was scarce in West Texas, and Walter couldn't spare a calf to butcher, so the meat in their diet was mostly salt pork. Hewey had to admit that Eve was a good cook, and she could do surprising things with salt pork, but it was still salt pork. It was becoming monotonous to one and all.

"Tommy and I saw a good hole of water in the draw the other day when we were cuttin' wood," Hewey said that morning at breakfast. "Bound to have some fish in it."

Eve cut Walter a sharp glance, but the boys were enthusiastic, and Walter found himself caught up in it.

"Won't take us long to find out," he said, "and we should be home early enough to break out a few more rows before dark. We're gettin' ahead, what with Hewey cuttin' posts and Cotton and me spendin' full time on the plow."

"Don't dawdle" was all Eve said, but she said it like she meant it. Hewey harbored no doubts that she did.

They set out early. Walter had dug some fish-hooks and twine out of a box in the barn, and they cut mesquite saplings for poles at the first draw they came to. They whittled the thorns and small branches as they rode, Tommy proudly using his new knife. Hewey could have done it for him in a fraction of the time, but he refrained, letting the youngster do it himself. The fishing was slow, but they gradually accumulated a few catfish on a stringer made of old fence wire. By early afternoon they had more than enough for a good meal.

"I reckon we'd best call it a day," said Walter. "I promised Eve we'd be back in time to get some work done."

They had just finished coiling up the twine when Alvin Lawdermilk's wagon rolled to a stop. His young Mexican hand, Julio, unhitched the team and led it to water.

"Sure glad to see the Calloways," said Alvin as he climbed down from the wagon. He was none too steady, and Hewey saw him pull a flat bottle out of the wagon bed. It was almost half empty, and Hewey had a good idea where the amber liquid had gone.

"Fishin' is thirsty work," Alvin pronounced loudly and with a slight slur. "Bet you men could use a drink."

"Don't mind if I do," Hewey answered.

Walter hesitated, but he, too, gave in to temptation.

"Much obliged, Alvin," he said, as he took a modest swig.

Hewey's swig hadn't been that modest. He noticed, though, that as Alvin passed the bottle a second and then a third round, Walter's modesty had begun to fade.

Soon Julio had the team hitched again, and Alvin turned back to the wagon. "Got some more miles to make," he said, handing the bottle in Hewey's general direction. "You boys finish the rest of it. You'll need it more than I do, and I can always dig up more."

Hewey knew Lawdermilk had bottles stashed all over his place, hidden from the prying eyes of the womenfolk. The two men finished the last of the bottle shortly before they rode up to the Calloway homestead.

"Well, boys, it's been a good day, and we're not even late," Walter said, his voice bearing a pronounced slur.

Eve knew even before they came close enough for her to smell them. She barely looked at the fish, and Hewey wished she hadn't looked so closely at him and Walter.

"Another afternoon's work shot," she said acidly.

Walter protested that there was still time to plow.

"In your condition you'd get a leg broken, and be no good to anybody. We'll eat when you get the fish cleaned. This day is done."

Walter and the boys melted away quickly, leaving Hewey to face Eve alone. He would have traded that opportunity for a barehanded bout with a panther.

"Nice mess of fish," he said lamely. "The boys done good."

"Looks like you and Walter did better," she said through gritted teeth.

"Now, Eve," he protested, "Walter needed a little break. A man can't live on work alone."

"How would you know?" she retorted. "I'm beginning to think you'll never settle down and take a wife. Probably just as well; you'd soon get a notion to run off on one of your irresponsible larks and leave her to fend for herself."

The words burned like sweat in a raw wound, and Hewey felt the color rising in his cheeks.

"I always try to pull my weight, and I still think it did Walter good to ease up a little," he argued. "He's gonna burn himself out."

"What would do Walter good would be for his fiddle-footed cowboy brother to ride on and let him make something of himself!" She was seething, and her eyes bored into Hewey's.

He thought of several sharp rejoinders, but realized the whisky might tempt him to say too much, so he set his jaw and kept those thoughts to himself.

Eve didn't say a word through supper, and Hewey saw that she barely touched her fish. He put his empty plate into the washtub and excused himself, retiring to the barn and wishing his legs were steady enough to take him farther. He hit his bedroll early but couldn't sleep, hearing Eve's words over and over: *"What would do Walter good would be for his fiddle-footed cowboy brother to ride on and let him make something of himself!"*

Eve's harsh words seared every time they ran through Hewey's head. What cut even deeper was the realization that they were largely true; Hewey often acted in haste, without care for the potential consequences. If a notion struck him, he did it, and devil take the hindmost.

Yes, Eve had him dead to rights, and no amount of rationalizing could change that.

Long before the others were up, he'd saddled Biscuit, tied his bedroll on, and was gone.

CHAPTER TWO

Alvin Lawdermilk's place bespoke of much more prosperity than the Calloway homestead. His ranch was not as large as C. C. Tarpley's in terms of acreage, but much of what C.C. operated was state lease, open to four-section claims by ambitious homesteaders. Alvin, by contrast, was secure in that he owned his land. No homesteader was going to push him off, and no bank would take it away.

He also took a broader view of ranching than did C.C. Whereas the Two Cs specialized in cattle, Alvin raised horses and mules for sale; the cattle more of a sideline. His headquarters was a livestock menagerie of sheep, goats, pigs, and peacocks. No intruder was going to sneak up on the place with that guard patrol of shrieking birds.

The peafowl announced Hewey's arrival. It was

still shy of daylight when he rode in, but Hewey knew the layout well. In addition to the large, two-story frame house, Alvin had several barns and an expanse of corrals to accommodate his horse and mule business. He got by well enough with the one hand, Julio, much of the time, but had built a decent bunkhouse for those periods when he took on extra help. Julio usually had it to himself.

An attached cookshack went largely unused because Julio ordinarily ate in the big house with the family. Alvin and Cora Lawdermilk held no more prejudice against Mexicans than Hewey, who judged a man by his actions rather than his accent or the shade of his skin. Old Lady Faversham wasn't prejudiced, either; she appeared to detest every one of the male persuasion equally. Alvin and Julio might retire to the cookshack for a few meals when she got on one of her particular tears, but otherwise it stood idle unless Alvin was working a crew too large for Cora's ample culinary skills.

This was one of those latter times. Still stinging from Eve's harsh dressing-down, Hewey reined up by the bunkhouse; he knew Alvin would be along directly if he wasn't already there. The smell of coffee and bacon wafted out to him as he loosened Biscuit's cinch. His stomach was uncertain after the previous day's alcohol and a sleepless night, but he told himself that breakfast would set things right.

"Mornin', Hooley," he called out as he entered the cookshack door. "Got enough for a fiddle-footed cowboy?"

"Come on in, Señor Hewey," a grinning Julio responded, wiping his hands on the flour sack he wore for an apron before reaching out to shake. "Always there is comida for you."

Hewey knew some of the cowboys at the table, and it didn't take long to make the acquaintance of the others. He remembered what Alvin had said earlier about having taken on a couple of knuckleheads, and he quickly picked them out of the group. One was tall and thin as a whippet hound, the other average height and well fed. They were crowding Julio and trying to eat what wasn't ready yet. A real hand showed the cook considerable deference, for an unhappy cook could lead to all sorts of miseries. The charitable view of their behavior was that they were fresh off the farm and knew little about cow-country etiquette. Hewey settled on a less charitable explanation: they were, indeed, knuckleheads.

Despite the interference, Julio soon pronounced breakfast ready, and the men took turns filing past the big iron stove, filling their tin plates with bacon, scrambled eggs, and Julio's Mexican-style flatbread. It wasn't biscuits, but Hewey remembered it as being good, better than a lot of biscuits he'd eaten, especially his own.

As a nonworking visitor, he waited for the hands to fill their plates ahead of him, and insisted that Julio go before him. Alvin had entered just before he got in line, and Hewey tried to wave him through after Julio, but Alvin pulled rank and insisted on bringing up the rear.

"I own this outfit and you're my guest, so git in line and fill your plate, Hewey."

It wasn't Hewey's first time to taste Julio's version of eggs, and he tried his best to avoid the red and green chunks scattered liberally throughout. He wasn't entirely successful, however, and soon wished he had something other than hot coffee with which to quench the fire in his mouth. The second batch didn't seem quite as hot, even though it came from the same big skillet. Hewey reckoned that his nerves had been cauterized.

When the other cowboys filed out to begin the day's work—the knuckleheads lagging behind—Alvin turned to Hewey.

"A pleasant surprise to see you, Hewey," he said. "Didn't expect you for another week or more, but I'm glad you're here. Now I can let them two chuck-line riders go."

"Hate to see a man lose a job on my account," Hewey protested, but mildly.

"It ain't on your account," Alvin answered, "but on their own no-account. So what brings you here ahead of schedule?"

"You remember us runnin' into you yesterday at that draw, and your hospitality?"

"'Course I do. Hope you and Walter enjoyed what was left in that bottle."

"Oh, we did that, Alvin, sure enough," Hewey said, "but later I discovered something I should have figured out a long time ago. Whisky and women do not mix."

"Hell, son, I could have told you that." Alvin laughed. "They're a fatal combination."

"Well, how have you managed?"

"Stealth and treachery, Hewey, stealth and treachery."

Alvin's parting of the ways with the two lazy hands, Wilkins and Pinch, left Hewey uneasy. They blustered, huffed, and puffed when the rancher cut them loose.

"I doubt this is the first time you two have been fired," Alvin told them in response.

"It sure ain't," the chubby one shot back, too pleased with himself to realize how dimwitted the reply had been.

The tall, thin one nodded his agreement. "But we ain't never been fired without so much as a fare-thee-well before." His fists were clenched and he moved toward Alvin in a menacing way.

"Then fare thee damn well," answered Alvin with a theatrical sweep of his hat. "Havin' you two around was like losin' half a dozen good hands."

It didn't help that several of the other hands had seen the exchange from a distance as they lounged in the shade of the bunkhouse porch. Most of them just snickered, but one with an irrepressible funny bone laughed out loud.

It appeared at one point as if they might come to blows with the gray-haired rancher, and Hewey was prepared to step in, as was Julio, who pulled a length of stove wood from the stack by the cook-house door.

After a bit more posturing and verbal fireworks, the inept cowboys collected their pay and headed for the horse lot, but Hewey didn't relax until they'd saddled their personal mounts and ridden off. Even then, he had a bad feeling. Their expressions bore a combustible mixture of humiliation and anger.

By noon Hewey had seen and heard enough about the string of fillies to conclude that only about a half dozen head still needed work. They were easy enough to keep track of: two sorrels, a gray, a line-backed dun, and a bloodred bay whose color Hewey considered appropriate. The well-built bay bared its teeth at any other horse that dared crowd it at the feed trough, and laid its ears back menacingly at the men in the corral.

Alvin saw Hewey eyeing the horse. "She's a fighter," he said. "Several of the boys have had a saddle on her, but none of 'em has stayed in it long enough to rub the dust out of the seat."

Hewey built a midsized loop in his rope, and with a fluid motion lofted it over the heads of the other fillies. He braced himself as the rope settled neatly over the bay's head. By the time she felt the pressure on her neck, Hewey had pulled the rope around behind him at hip level, set his heels, and leaned against it. The herd parted quickly as the bay filly sat back against the restraint. When the rope tightened around her neck, she fought it briefly, then put her ears back and charged.

Hewey was momentarily surprised by her reaction to the rope, but seized the advantage afforded by the sudden slack and moved quickly to the stout snubbing post set deeply in the center of the pen. He flipped a coil of rope over the post, and as she came at him, reeled in the line. The bay was snubbed tight before she knew what had happened. With Julio's help Hewey slipped a braided rope hackamore over her head and snugged it. The halter-like headgear was mostly a contrivance to anchor a hard-rope noseband with a large knot at the bottom, where the reins were fastened; it tilted forward on top and backward under the horse's jawbone when the rider drew on the reins. The combined pressure from above on its nose and from below on the sensitive jawbone tended to get the animal's attention and encourage cooperation. Hewey then added his blanket and saddle between crow-hops. It took him two tries to grab his cinch and thread the leather latigo strap through the ring on his rigging. After a couple of wraps of the latigo through the saddle ring and cinch ring he tightened it and fastened the tongue.

Julio had dallied the long hackamore lead known as a mecate—Anglicized by most cowboys to "McCarty"—and pulled the bay tighter against the snubbing post, leaving enough slack in the catch rope for Hewey to loosen the loop from her neck and slip it off her head. Once Hewey had both of the thick rope reins in his left hand, Julio doubled the nearest ear over and bit down on it, distracting the filly long enough for Hewey to step up into the saddle. At a nod from Hewey, he jerked the slip-knot in the mecate and turned her loose.

It was a performance that townfolk would pay good money to see at the Pecos Rodeo, but it ended up with Hewey facedown in the dirt. At least he'd stayed long enough to put a shine on the seat of his saddle. A couple of Alvin's cowboys caught the bay and snubbed her again. Once Hewey's head cleared and he could see one rather than two fillies, he stepped aboard. It took three tries—and two rough landings—before Hewey fought the bay to a quivering stand.

"I think she's had enough for today," he announced hoarsely.

Julio took a firm and close hold on the trailing mecate while Hewey dismounted and unsteadily removed his saddle and blanket. He then pulled the slipknot in the hackamore and freed the bay's head. She backed quickly away, stopped, shook herself, and sucked air.

"It ain't right," Hewey said when Alvin Lawdermilk told him how much he would pay for the trailing job.

Alvin looked startled. "What do you mean, it ain't right?"

"C.C. never paid me more than a dollar a day,

and you're offerin' to pay me a dollar and a half. I'd feel like a highway robber takin' it."

"Well, Hewey," Alvin answered, "C. C. Tarpley has his standards and I have mine. Your helper gets a buck and a quarter, in case you're wonderin'."

"Then why don't I be the helper and you get somebody else to be the boss? I'd a lot rather be the wrangler than the ramrod, with all that responsibility. You could get anybody you wanted at your price."

"Yes, and I want you. Hewey, I've never seen anybody take to the cowboy life like you do. Any ideas who you'd like to take with you?"

"I'd take Walter, but Eve'd shoot me just for suggestin' it. She's not in a good humor with me anyway. Young Cotton could sure use an adventure, but Eve'd shoot me twice for that. Grady Welch is runnin' the wagon for C.C., and I've got no notion where Snort Yarnell is. Maybe one of your boys? There's some good hands among 'em."

"I've already quizzed them and got no takers, but there are a couple of other possibilities. An older fellow has been droppin' in pretty regular, hopin' for the job, and some young kid."

"An old feller?"

"Not old, just older. He's an acquaintance of Wes Wheeler from years ago."

"Sheriffs get acquainted with lots of people, mostly people who're kinda casual about right and wrong."

"I get a strong impression this one wore a badge, just like Wes."

"I'd rather not nursemaid a pensioner, Alvin. I need somebody young enough to keep up with me."

"I figured he could supply the experience and you could supply the youth—what you've still got of it. I don't suppose you've spent too much time in front of a mirror lately, have you?"

Alvin had cut right to the heart of something that had been nagging Hewey for a while, something he couldn't quite put his finger on. Now that he knew what it was, it burned a little.

"Then I reckon I need to run with the young dogs one more time before I take to my rocker," Hewey said, with an edge to his voice that surprised even him.

"I didn't mean anything by that remark, Hewey. You've still got a lot of young in you. But you're the one makin' the trip; you take whoever you want."

"I want the kid. Does he have a name?"

"Never been very good with names, Hewey," Alvin said. "Show me a horse and I'll remember every mark on him, but a man's name . . ." He paused, deep in thought. "Brindle, bridle . . . Bradley. That's it, Billy Joe Bradley."

Later that afternoon, Hewey had decided that the young horses knew about all they could learn in the classroom; between being trailed and being ridden, they would get their higher education on the way to Colorado. The bay would be his own special pupil.

"Your name Hewey Calloway?"

"It was the last time I looked." Hewey was in the saddle barn, turning his sweat-soaked blanket upside down over the seat of his saddle so it could air. He stepped outside to see who was asking. It was the kid.

"I hear you're takin' some horses to Colorado, and need another man. I'd be right tickled to have the job. Been wantin' to see Colorado again for a long time."

Sizing him up, Hewey doubted he'd been doing anything for a very long time. He looked younger than Hewey had expected. It gave him pause.

"The pay wouldn't be much," he answered, thinking, *But better than I've ever made*.

"I ain't lookin' to get rich," Billy Joe Bradley responded with a lopsided grin. "I'm just lookin' to get away from this mesquite and greasewood and these piddlin' little hills they call mountains around here. I want to see some real mountains again."

Hewey hadn't made up his mind, and was noncommittal. "Colorado's got 'em."

"You been there?" the kid asked.

"Not yet."

"Well, I have, so I know my way around. I'd be a guide as well as a wrangler."

An older man had appeared in the background, by the horse lot gate. Hewey could see that he wanted to talk but was reluctant to intrude.

"I'll let you know, kid."

Billy Joe Bradley gave the older man a glance, then flashed Hewey a toothy grin and turned away. Hewey thought the expression fell somewhere between confident and cocky, weighted a bit toward the latter—and lesser—attitude. He gave the older man a long glance, not quite an invitation.

"My name's Hanley Baker," the man said as he walked up, extending a hand that felt like a hickory knot. "Alvin tells me you're fixin' to drive a string of horses up to the Durango country for him."

Hewey acknowledged. "I am." He closed the saddle house door and stepped away. The two men walked as they talked.

"I know my way around up there. Lived north of Durango for several years. Still have a cabin, if it ain't fallen in."

Hewey noticed a significant catch in the older man's gait, a limp that Baker made no effort to hide. *Lots of things tend to fall in with age*, he thought.

"Just speaks for a lifetime of experience," Baker said with a smile, obviously reading Hewey's eyes if not his thoughts. "I can still hold my own, if that's a concern."

"I'm not concerned," Hewey answered. It wasn't exactly a lie. The older man was beginning to impress him, the younger one less so. "You and the kid are both anglin' for the same job. I ain't quite decided."

"Take your time. Alvin's invited us both to stay for supper."

Julio's cooking was good, as usual, and spicy, but Hewey ate more by habit than with his customary relish. He was deep in thought. He'd told Alvin he was ready to leave at first light, eager to get an early start on a trip he could only vaguely map out, with little clear notion just how long it would take or what it would entail. He'd also told Alvin he had made his choice about a partner, but now he was having second thoughts. The kid was younger than he'd envisioned, and if anything, acted even less mature than he looked. Hanley Baker, on the other hand, had begun to grow on him.

Alvin was in his small, book-lined office when Hewey went to see him.

"I reckon I need to tell them two job-seekers what I've decided," he said to Alvin. "One of 'em needs to know he ain't goin' to Colorado." He was stalling.

"You want me to call 'em in here?" Alvin asked.

"No need. I'll go to them. It's up to me to do."

"Well, while you're here, I'd like to bounce an idea off of you. How about you let me send Julio and the boys on ahead with the horses, just for three or four days, to get 'em off of familiar country and into a trail routine?"

"I don't see any of 'em makin' trouble," Hewey said, "outside of that hardheaded bay, anyway."

"At that age you never can tell for sure what they're goin' to do," Alvin responded. "Besides, you need to provision, and prices are better in Midland than in Upton City. Lay around here a day or two, get a little of that vacation you still ain't had time for, then swing by Midland with one of those fillies for a packhorse. You'll travel some faster than the boys can push that herd at first, catch up to 'em in no time. The extra boys could use a few more days' pay before I have to lay 'em off."

It sounded like a good idea to Hewey, even more so when he recalled Alvin's run-in with the two laggards. He was a little concerned about leaving him and the womenfolk alone, though he would never let on.

"You've got a deal."

Hewey was still debating his choice as he left Alvin's office, but he'd settled on a decision by the time he reached the bunkhouse. He saw Hanley Baker first.

"I've made up my mind," he said to the older man.

"I can tell by the set of your jaw what you've decided," Baker answered. "Don't let that spook you," he continued. "I've had years of experience readin' men, and it's allowed me to get as old as I have. I spent a long time in a line of work that didn't tolerate misreadin' another man's intentions."

"I've never been in a position to tell a man yea or nay about a job, except my own," Hewey said. "I'm not sure I feel real comfortable with it."

"You've done fine," Baker said. "No hard feelin's on my part. I had the sense you'd made your mind up before we met, but afterward you gave me full consideration, and that's all a man can ask."

Hewey's conversation with Billy Joe Bradley was less satisfying. He could take bragging in stride, and had done his share of it—always justified, of course. What he never much held with was gloating, and Billy Joe Bradley came close to the line.

After a cut for soundness and quality, Alvin's official count came to seventy-two head, and Julio assured Hewey that the patron had been sober when he made it. Hewey was determined to deliver precisely that many to the buyer.

He felt odd, standing there holding the gate while his herd spilled out, heading north under the care of a crew of cowboys that didn't include him. The fillies kicked, bucked, and cavorted like a bunch of colts on a frosty morning. The sight was pleasing, even if it didn't feel quite right.

He went back to the cookshack for another cup of Julio's leftover coffee, feeling at loose ends. There was Hanley Baker, tying his bedroll down.

"About that job . . ." Hewey began.

"You've got nothing to apologize for," Baker assured him with an easy smile. Hewey hadn't quite realized that's what he was trying to do. "Alvin offered me a few days' work helpin' start those horses, but Wes Wheeler has some odds and ends he wants a hand with, so I declined. Hope we run into each other again sometime."

Not sure quite what prompted him, Hewey said, "Mr. Baker, I'd appreciate it if you'd let Wes Wheeler know about somethin'. Alvin let a couple of useless cowboys go a few days ago and they looked like they were goin' to gang up on him, they were so mad. I think they would have if there hadn't been a bunch of us there to stop 'em. Once I leave, there'll just be Alvin and the womenfolk for a couple or three days, and I'm uneasy about it."

"Thanks for the heads-up," Baker answered. "I'll pass that on to Wes, and nose around a little on my own, too." He swung into the saddle, extended his hand to shake, and rode away in the direction of Upton City.

Hewey felt relieved to be sharing the burden of his suspicions.

Two days of idleness were all Hewey could stand. The third morning he had saddled Biscuit, tied his bedroll on, and caught the filly he'd held back for a packhorse. After securing the pack frame with its small camp kit and tarp, he mounted Biscuit and led the filly up to Alvin's office.

"I have a little cash here to get you started, Hewey, but I want you to draw as much as you think you'll need at the First National Bank in Midland."

"I could be just anybody. How would they know to believe me?"

"I have a letter here to the bank president authorizing him to draw on my account. If you'll get him to sign it, too, you should be able to present it at almost any bank along the way in case you run short. They can wire the request, and a lot of 'em have telephones now. The world is runnin' faster and faster every day."

Hewey rough counted the bills Alvin had handed him. "I could make it most of the way on this by itself. I travel pretty light."

"When a man works for me, I feed him," Alvin answered. "It's a point of pride. You can get your first provisions at Simpson's store. I have an account there. Show the letter if you need to."

Outside, Hewey lifted his bedroll enough to open his near-side saddlebag and deposit the money and letter. As he buckled the flap back down, Alvin interrupted him.

"Hang on, Hewey, I nearly forgot." Alvin went back into his office and returned with another letter and a small map. "My buyer's name is McKenzie. Runs a decent-sized horse operation in that Durango country. He sent this map and directions on how to get ahold of him."

Military man, Hewey thought when he saw the map. It reminded him of some of the Army maps he'd seen during his brief foray with Teddy Roosevelt in Cuba. That experience gave him an abundance of material for stories, most of them at least reasonably true. Some people scoffed when he told them that Colonel Teddy had spoken to him personally, but he had. Mounted on one of the few horses that had made the trip, Roosevelt reviewed his volunteer corps of cowboys and adventurers one morning. On the way down the line, he stopped directly in front of Hewey, looked him square in the eye through those little pinch-nose glasses, and said, "Button that collar, soldier."

Inside the cloth sack under the map and directions, Alvin had secreted one of his many samples of Kentucky's finest. "For medicinal purposes," he said with a wink when Hewey noticed the bottle. Hewey added that to the saddlebag, then put his left foot in the stirrup and swung lightly into the saddle. The two men exchanged handshakes and Hewey pointed Biscuit toward Midland.

He was off to see new country.

Early that afternoon Alvin Lawdermilk was kicked back in a chair on the porch. He had an open book in his lap but was gazing absentmindedly over his reading glasses at the empty pens when Hanley Baker rode up.

"Looks like I missed Calloway," he said as he dismounted. "Sure wish I'd caught him. There's somethin' he needs to know."

Baker told Alvin of Hewey's concerns about the two knuckleheads. "I came to tell him that he needn't worry about them showin' up here. Looks like they have business with him, not you."

"What would they want with Hewey?" Alvin asked.

"They're aiming to rob him," Baker replied. "They

were in Dutch Schneider's saloon last night, havin' a few shots of courage. Over all the noise, Schneider heard them goin' on about Calloway and that horse herd, and he passed it on to Wes Wheeler this morning. I paid a call on Wes a little later, and that's when he told me. Schneider said those two were talkin' about a third partner, but they're the only cowboys in town that nobody knows."

"There was a third, all right," Alvin said, his face suddenly pinched with concern. "He's with Hewey."

"I'm of the same mind," Baker agreed.

"You still in need of a job?" Alvin asked.

CHAPTER THREE

The Two Cs' wagon was on the move almost daily that time of year, and Hewey spotted it off to his east shortly after noon. He angled that direction, hoping to pick up a free meal and a brief visit with Grady Welch and the hands. As he neared the site, he could tell the cowboys were already scattered for the afternoon. C. C. Tarpley preferred to see his hands working at all reasonable hours and some hours that weren't so reasonable. A figure he recognized as Shorty Jenkins, the cook, was bent over the washtub. As he heard the rider's approach, Jenkins peered out from under the generous brim of his grease-stained hat. Recognizing Hewey, he waved him in.

"You're just in time, Hewey," the cook said. "I was about to throw the last of the coffee out. The boys left a few biscuits and a dab of beef, and the beans ain't cold yet."

Hewey dismounted a respectful distance from the wagon so as not to stir up dust, tied the pack-horse's lead rope to his saddle horn, and dropped Biscuit's reins; the brown horse would stand where the reins fell, as surely as if he'd been tied.

"Well, Shorty, I see ol' C.C. ain't gotten any more tolerant about the crew dawdlin' over the noon meal." Hewey knew where to find a cup, plate, and fork, and served himself from the meager leftovers.

"C.C. ain't got any more tolerant about anything." Jenkins laughed. "Best eat all that meat; he gets purty religious about wastin' food, likes it to run out just before the last hand gets a full plate. Guess I miscalculated a bit this time."

"My good fortune that you did," Hewey answered with a chuckle.

The two exchanged news as Hewey ate and the cook worked. One thing they didn't discuss was Hewey's plans; it wasn't considered polite to inquire into a man's business if he didn't offer, and Hewey didn't offer. He considered mentioning his newly inflated pay scale, knowing it would eventually get back to Tarpley and rankle him a bit, but then he decided the skinflint wouldn't believe it anyway. He wasn't even sure Shorty Jenkins would believe it. In fact, he wasn't quite certain he believed it himself.

❖

Hewey had said everything that came into his head that morning a few weeks back. Some of those things were probably better left unsaid, as were some of the things C.C. had said to him. The two of them had always had a tendency to go a little overboard toward each other when things came to a head. They always got over it eventually. Nevertheless, about midafternoon he knew he was going to have to say something pretty soon; off in the distance he spotted C.C.'s buggy angling in his direction. He reined up and waited.

"I see you ain't left the country yet," the rancher said as he pulled alongside.

"Just fixin' to," Hewey responded. "Headed north to see some new country, and I ain't coming back until I'm rich and famous."

"Well, then, I reckon we won't see you for some time," Tarpley said with more than a little sarcasm in his voice. He flipped the reins at his team and moved on. Neither man looked back at the other.

It was late afternoon when Hewey reached Midland. The bank was closed and Simpson's store looked to be in the middle of a last-minute rush of customers. He stopped in at the wagonyard, arranged to spend the night in an empty stall, and turned the filly loose in a small pen. Stacking his gear and bedroll in the stall, he put Alvin's cash in his pocket for safekeeping, mounted Biscuit, and rode up the street, looking for supper.

Cowboy wages were better suited to a chili parlor than to a café with tablecloths, so that's where he went. After a spicy meal augmented with a goodly supply of free soda crackers, Hewey made one last stop at a familiar saloon. Normally he could count on seeing several cowboys he knew there, but the spring works were underway throughout the country, and cowboys at loose ends were scarce. He had two drinks at the mostly deserted bar, then remounted for the short ride back to the wagonyard. He fed Biscuit and the filly a bait of oats and a couple of chips of grass hay just as the sun set, and by dark he was sound asleep.

Daylight found him back at the chili parlor, where breakfast consisted of eggs with almost as much fire as Julio's huevos but without much of the flavor. The biscuits were decent, the bacon chewy but passable, and the gravy copious because flour and bacon grease were relatively cheap. All in all, it was a gourmet repast stacked up against Hewey's own cooking, and he knew he would soon be condemned to weeks of that regrettable fare. He got his money's worth, and was waiting outside Simpson's store before the doors opened. The bank was next, and despite Hewey's discomfort, the business there went smoothly. Alvin Lawdermilk's name carried some weight. Hewey was out of town and heading northwest before the sun had risen far in the eastern sky.

He caught up with the herd at the Seminole wells by early evening.

"You boys can leave it to me and the kid now," he said to the first cowboy he encountered, a hand he knew only as Skeeter. "Get yourselves a good night's sleep, then head south in the morning."

"The kid ain't here, Hewey," said Skeeter as Julio loped up to greet him.

"What? Where the hell is he?" Hewey swiveled his head, looking in all directions.

"Back in Midland, I think, Señor Hewey," answered Julio. "He said he had business before he goes. I tell him stay, but he says he takes no order from a Mexican."

"Didn't seem inclined to take much direction from us gringos, either," added Skeeter.

The kid went down another three notches in Hewey's estimation, one for leaving the job and two for sassing Julio. Hewey suddenly had a twinge of misgiving about his choice in partners. Misgivings weren't unusual, but they generally didn't happen until after a wreck.

Billy Joe Bradley showed up just after breakfast the next morning. As he kicked his right foot out of the stirrup, Hewey said sharply, "Don't bother to dismount. We've got a lot of miles to make before dark, and Julio and the boys are goin' home."

He saw something akin to pain in the kid's eyes as he watched Hewey deliberately pour the last of the coffee out on the fire. Julio did his best to stifle a smile.

"A day without breakfast can be hard on a workin' man," Hewey said by way of rubbing it in. "Behooves him to be where he ought to be on time."

Hewey pushed the fillies a little harder than he should have the first several days, and he knew it. He was really pushing the kid, and the fillies just got caught in the net. He finally lightened up; it was still a stretch to the Pecos, the way they were angling in on it. Hewey had considered cutting west through a leg of the deep sand to tire the young horses and take some of the vinegar out of them, but that had proved unnecessary. They settled to trailing fairly quickly, which Hewey attributed by and large to Alvin Lawdermilk's good bloodlines and gentle handling. What foolishness there had been he left mainly to the kid, hoping the vigorous activity would take a little of the starch out of him, too.

Instead, they stayed east of the sand, working northward as they edged west. Where the deep sand played out was a sharp caprock, the extreme western edge of the vast Llano Estacado. He didn't trust the fillies to safely navigate a steep descent on a narrow trail, and was edging toward an area where the caprock gave way briefly to a gentler slope. Hewey knew the lay of the land from working that country in the past. It had been a while, but the land didn't change. What had changed was brought about by human intervention. Fences had appeared where he remembered none. They cut trails that Hewey had known, forcing long detours. He considered fences a scourge in the main, but with them usually came waterings where Mother Nature had failed to provide; that part met with Hewey's approval.

The long trail along the Pecos was mostly uneventful, save the times when Hewey schooled the bay. The kid offered to take over the filly's education the first two times that Hewey raised himself from the ground and beat the dust from his hat. Hewey answered both offers with a glare that would kill a mesquite tree. The kid didn't ask a third time. As the days passed, Hewey began to read the filly's pattern, and increasingly matched her efforts with his own countermeasures. He slowly sensed the emergence of a saddle horse within the recalcitrant raw material. She never quit resisting, however, displaying a rebellious streak that he came to appreciate.

It was a puzzlement to Hewey just why the filly's stubbornness pleased him. He was pretty sure he had none of that trait in his own makeup.

The Pecos was swollen with snowmelt from distant mountains to the west and north, as it was every spring unless the winter had been dry. Hewey drifted the herd northward along the east bank of the river. He spoke to Billy Joe Bradley only when necessary, and his notion of necessary became more spare by the mile. The kid found it impossible to tease out a conversation and only a bit easier to pry loose any response at all.

"Hey, Calloway," he said one evening when they had brought the horses to a halt for the day, "where do you plan to cross this herd?"

"Outside Roswell," Hewey answered. That was his entire answer.

"Why not here, or anywhere in the last forty miles?"

"There's a bridge at Roswell."

"I thought you were supposed to be a cowboy," the kid fired back, "not a store clerk afraid to get his feet wet."

Bradley clearly knew nothing about the Pecos. With its steep banks and quicksand traps, it could be treacherous at low flow and downright deadly on a rise.

"I'm crossin' the herd at Roswell. You're welcome to wade in anywhere it pleases you, but leave your horse with me. I won't watch a damn fool drown a good mount." The subject was closed.

The multi-span bridge outside Roswell was visible from several miles away. Hewey had discovered it on his last sojourn into New Mexico, and it was still new enough that the paint on its steel frame hadn't weathered much. The pride of Roswell, it had tamed the capricious Pecos by soaring above the river and ignoring it. Hewey had to admit, if only to himself, that not every modern development deserved to be condemned.

As they approached the bridge, Hewey held the horses up and let them mill around and settle.

"What're you waitin' for, Calloway?" Billy Joe Bradley yelled across the herd. "You're slow as an old maid!"

"If you'd do more thinkin' and less goin' off half cocked, the world would be a better place, at least the part I'm in." That was all Hewey planned to say about the matter.

He retrieved a rope halter with a long lead from the pack mare, then eased out a bigger loop in his rope, took it in hand, and worked his way quietly to the center of the herd, sidling up to a sorrel he'd long had his eye on. Even back at Alvin's, she'd always taken the point, the first one into the corrals when the horse rustler brought them from the horse trap a little before daylight and the first one out when Alvin opened the gate of an evening. She also led the herd on the move, reserved the best patch of grass when they stopped, and when they bedded at night, she worked her way into the center of the herd, the safest spot in the event the horses were approached by wolves or other predators. She was nothing remarkable to look at, but she topped the pecking order, and none of the others challenged her, not even the bay.

Hewey slipped the loop of his rope over her head, and pulled her up close. She was gentle and didn't fight him, and he haltered her, removed his rope, then led her toward the bridge. The others followed.

"You bring up the drag and do it slow and easy," he told the kid, voiced in the form of an order. "Them wooden planks on the bridge are gonna be a little spooky for these girls, and I don't want a runaway."

Mounted on Biscuit and with the lead filly in tow, Hewey had his end of the crossing nailed down tight. The kid was the only wild card in the deck, and he was the Joker.

As Hewey's mount struck the bridge, the hoofbeats rang out, and the lead horse balked. Biscuit himself took it in stride, so Hewey wrapped a couple of dallies around the saddle horn with the halter lead and moved on. The filly reluctantly yielded, but her first steps onto the boards caused her to freeze and set back against the lead rope. Hewey stopped briefly but kept the pressure on.

Finally the filly gave in again and gingerly set all four feet on the bridge. Her ears were cocked forward and her eyes wide, so Hewey gave her plenty of time to assess the situation. Then he moved forward slowly. The filly rolled her eyes to see the iron framework as it closed in on both sides of her and crisscrossed overhead; her neck was stretched forward and her head immobilized by the pull of the lead rope, but she could see the shadows, and they were scary. Hewey took it slow, looking back at the lead horse and watching for followers.

He was about a fourth of the way across when

a filly, seeing the leader moving off without her, stepped onto the bridge deck. She took small, mincing steps, but she was coming. Then a second horse, a third, and a lengthening line of others. They came single file at first, then by twos and threes. Hewey turned his attention toward the far end of the bridge, where he half expected some town dweller to show up with a wagon or a hack and ball the whole thing up. None appeared, and Hewey could see nothing approaching. He soon realized he'd had his shoulders hunched and his neck tensed; it took a conscious effort to relax the knots. Looking back again, he could see almost the entire herd on the bridge, skittish and nervous, but coming along. He smiled to himself.

By then he was almost to the end. The road took a sharp turn to the right after the bridge, and Hewey strained to see where the steep embankment began to level out. He would settle the herd there for a while before moving on. The thought struck him that getting so close to a big town like Roswell but passing by without stopping would chap Billy Joe Bradley severely. Hewey saw no downside to that.

He was just turning back for another look when he heard the kid whoop and holler and saw him waving his hat. In an instant the horses broke into a high lope, bouncing off the guardrails and closing the distance at a frightening pace. The bridge vibrated, hoofbeats turned into a constant roll of thunder, and Hewey spurred Biscuit forward. He had just time to feel the tug of the halter rope on the lead mare before she was suddenly beside him and surging.

They cleared the bridge in a few bounds, but the lead horse was blocking him on the right and he couldn't make the turn. He pitched the rope to her and took a deep seat as he and Biscuit plunged off the roadbed onto the steep embankment. Biscuit was airborne for what seemed like half an hour before he landed well down the steep slope. The impact was hard, and the rider-burdened horse was overbalanced forward. His forelegs went out from under him, his head went down, and Hewey felt himself rising out of his stirrups.

With all the strength in both arms, Hewey sat back and hauled up on the reins. Biscuit's head came up, he regained his footing, and he got in one more lunge before level ground came up fast to meet them. That time Biscuit went to his knees for just an instant before other horses came down around them, many tumbling and lashing out with their hooves, trying to find purchase. Hewey's teeth clattered together but he never lost his seat, and soon he and Biscuit were out on open ground, trying to put space between themselves and the other horses.

The horses had the same idea, and scattered in all directions, most of them trying to get as far as possible from that evil bridge. They wouldn't quit running for a while, and Hewey guessed it would take a full day or more to find all of them in the salt cedar and other brush along the river. Some might even end up in town. Those he'd seen all appeared to be traveling on four legs; they couldn't have covered that much ground so fast on three. Still, he hated to think about it, but it would be a miracle if some of them didn't have broken legs.

Horses, like people, are all individuals with their own temperaments. Some of the fillies had followed the roadbed and clustered together on open ground a hundred or so yards to the north. They'd had time to settle and get over the shakes, unlike those that were likely still running. These horses were the more levelheaded of the band, and would form the nucleus of the herd; some of the others would join them after they quit running and began to filter back. Many, of course, would have to be found and driven back.

Hewey wasn't surprised to see that the bay mare was among the levelheaded batch. He knew that she had a thinking nature about her, because she was always plotting new ways to unseat him.

Billy Joe Bradley spurred his horse down the embankment and loped up to Hewey, his face flushed with excitement and a big grin on his face.

"Damn, Calloway, that was a helluva wreck!"

Bradley was laughing by then, and Hewey felt his right hand reaching for the saddle gun in its scabbard. He struggled to stop himself, an effort that probably was harder than it should have been.

"What in God's name did you think you were doing?" he thundered.

"Some of them gals were lollygaggin' around and didn't want to cross, so I choused 'em a little, that's all." He was still chuckling, and Hewey felt that urge again. . . .

"I really oughta shoot you out of the saddle. Not a jury in cow country would convict me. Now, get over the chuckles and start huntin' horses. You'll go north and I'll go south. I hope one of us finds the packhorse, or it'll be a hungry camp tonight."

"Hell, Calloway, we can go to town and have a real meal, with decent cookin'."

"You go if you want to—afoot and carrying your saddle, because you aren't comin' back here."

"I come with a horse, and when I go, I'll go with a horse," Bradley snapped back.

"Not that one. It's one of mine. Yours is amongst the runaways."

The kid glared at Hewey, reined his horse to the right, and loped off upriver, spooking some of the remaining fillies as he plowed through them. Hewey turned downriver. He could tell Biscuit was favoring his near front leg. It was faint, but Hewey knew how the brown horse traveled, and it didn't feel quite right. He considered roping a fresh mount out of the cluster that stayed put, but decided that a little slow, light travel might work the kink out before it turned into sure-enough lameness. He promised himself they'd go easy.

He found the packhorse before he'd gone far. Over her fright by then, she was picking at a small patch of short grass. He found two more, then another three. About half a mile from the bridge he found a full dozen. That was far enough for Biscuit, he figured, so he eased around the bunch and nudged them northward, picking up the others as they went. When they came in sight of the bigger group, one of the strays nickered loudly, and Hewey heard a response. Soon they struck a long trot, eager to rejoin their herd-mates. They gave wide roundance to the bridge as they passed it, Hewey noticed. He kept Biscuit in his customary long-strided walk, not wanting to take any chances. When he got near enough to give the herd a rough count, Hewey saw that it was larger than when he'd left; a few more strays had evidently drifted back in while he was gone. It was a good start.

Hewey eased around the little herd and positioned himself a few hundred yards to the north. He suspected the kid would come in at a lope, driving whatever he found at much too fast a pace, and he was determined to slow them down before they scattered the whole outfit again.

He was right.

It took most of the next day to round up the remainder, but eventually Hewey got his full count. Some of them were scratched up and a dozen or so gimped a little, but none were crippled. With a couple of hours of daylight remaining, he put the horses back on the trail, aiming to leave a few miles between them and Roswell before they stopped. Several times he saw Billy Joe Bradley gazing back longingly toward the receding town, and took pleasure—just a little—in the kid's discomfort. He hadn't spoken a word to him since the bridge, and didn't plan to until he needed to give an order.

"Who's out there?" Hewey demanded, straining his eyes to peer into the darkness beyond the feeble glow of his small campfire.

"Keep your voice down, Calloway," came a whisper from the dark.

Hewey judged the odds of reaching his carbine, and moved slightly in that direction. He heard "Stay put, cowboy. There's no call for foolishness."

Feeling helpless, Hewey watched a form emerge from the darkness. Squinting, he could make out a limp and the face of the older hand he'd left behind at Alvin Lawdermilk's place.

"I've had a feeling somebody was doggin' me," Hewey said.

"You have good instincts for a cowboy," said Hanley Baker as he moved in closer. "You're bein' followed, all right," Baker continued, "but I'm not the only dog on your trail. Mind givin' me a sip of that coffee? I haven't had any in days. Those two chuckline riders that Alvin let go have been after you since Midland. Your green hand met 'em at the hotel, and he's been slipping off to parley with 'em most every night on his watch."

"Do they know you're watchin' them watch me?"

"A man doesn't see me unless I want him to, and so far it has not pleased my fancy to make an appearance."

"So what the hell are you up to? Seems like an awful long pleasure ride to me."

"Alvin had some doubts about your choice in partners. I've been on his payroll just like you."

"Damn that old horse trader!" Hewey shook his fist. "I don't need a nursemaid."

"No, but you could sure as hell use a guardian angel, and I'm it. Those boys are bent on robbin' you, in case you haven't figured it out."

"At three against one, they could take these horses any time they wanted to, so what are they waitin' for?"

"They don't want the horses, Hewey; that'd be work, and most thieves are born naturally lazy. They figure to let you do all the heavy liftin', and then relieve you of the burden of Alvin's money."

"Ah, I hadn't thought of that angle."

"That's because you're not lazy, and you're not a thief. Now I need to slip back out of here in case the kid cuts his watch short and tries to cheat you out of a little sleep. Just thought it was high time you knew what you were up against."

"Why don't I just give the kid his time and you take his place? I should've picked you to start with."

"Calloway, you really do think like an honest man, don't you? If I showed myself and went with you, who would be watchin' them? No, it's better this way."

"What can I do to help?"

"Just keep on the way you're goin', and pretend we haven't had this talk." Baker took a couple of steps, then stopped and turned back. "On second thought, you could bed those horses some earlier on occasion, and leave me a little daylight to build a fire. I'm gettin' damn tired of makin' a cold camp every night."

"You can't gather wood in the dark?"

"There you go thinkin' like an honest man again. Those two aren't very bright, but they could spot a fire at night. I can sure as hell see theirs."

Hewey settled into a pattern of avoiding the few towns he encountered, even if it meant a detour. He still had plenty of provisions, and it annoyed the kid, which pleased the contrary side of Hewey's nature. Eventually, he was challenged.

"I've seen towns, but only at a distance," the kid complained one day. "I sure would like to see one closer up."

"I haven't forgotten that stunt you pulled on the boys at Midland. Went off and left 'em."

"I told that Mex I had business."

Hewey now knew what kind of business that had been, but he wasn't about to let on. "Take it from a wise elder, chasin' skirts will get you into trouble. My brother chased one until she caught him, and he's had a pair of plow handles stuck to his palms ever since. Besides, towns attract people, and people build fences. The goin's easier where there aren't any."

Hewey touched spurs lightly to Biscuit and rode off, determined to make that the last word. He was getting under the kid's skin, and he enjoyed it.

Another habit he settled into was worrying. What Hanley Baker had said made sense. It stood to reason that the kid and his accomplices would wait until Hewey had money to steal instead of horses. Still, Hewey couldn't be sure. It got to where he lay awake through most of the kid's night shift when he could have been sleeping, and it was beginning to wear on him, along with the weight of responsibility he hadn't wanted to begin with. He was harder on the horses than he knew he should be, and once he even found himself reining Biscuit the way he would a cold-jawed horse, something he never would have done under normal circumstances.

He was hard on the kid, too, but that didn't bother Hewey one bit.

By this point in the journey, Hewey's almost daily schooling of the bay had become routine, so he expected nothing out of the ordinary when it came time for the bay's next lesson, but she'd saved a trick or two, and it took only one of them to catch him off guard. He remembered a brief sensation of flight, which ended abruptly when he slammed into the ground. It took him a few seconds to raise his head, and in that brief interval the bay had wheeled and run. The kid was hard on her heels, shaking out a loop as he went. In no time the rope was around the filly's neck and Bradley reined left, pitching the slack as he turned. Like most cowboys, he had the rope tied hard and fast to the saddle horn.

Hewey saw the wreck coming but lacked the breath to say anything. The young cowboy spurred his mount and leaned away from the jerk that came when the bay hit the end of the rope with both horses going in opposite directions. She reared straight up and fell backward. Then she lay still. Even from his vantage point, Hewey knew she was dead; died within seconds of having her neck snapped when she hit the end of that unyielding rope. This was no crippled horse that would need to be put down. Billy Joe Bradley had seen to that. A skilled hangman could hardly have been more thorough.

There had only been two possible outcomes to the kid's reckless move, and Hewey found himself wishing that Bradley's mount had gone down instead, and it had been the kid who wouldn't get up again. The thought startled him, and he was even more surprised to realize that he meant every unspoken word of it. Still breathless, Hewey ran through his entire vocabulary of cuss words in his head. By then the kid had retrieved his rope and ridden back to where Hewey was coming to his feet.

"She shoulda yielded when she felt the rope," he

said, and Hewey was furious to see a trace of a smile on the kid's face.

"You never gave her a chance," Hewey spat back. "She comes out of your pay. Kill another one, and you won't have any pay."

Once he left familiar country behind, Hewey began to rely more and more on the map he'd gotten from Alvin. The thought of asking the kid for directions galled him, so he did the best he could on his own. The map was detailed enough to leave little room for doubt. Days passed, and Durango drew closer. One morning he saw a rider approaching. He had sent the kid up ahead to ride point, and as the stranger drew near, Hewey saw the kid gesture back in his direction. The rider eased around the herd and extended a hand as Hewey pulled even with him.

"Name's Rutherford," the man said, "Trace Rutherford. I ride for Major Bryce McKenzie, and we've been expecting you."

"Hewey Calloway," Hewey replied. "Where can we hold these girls until you take delivery?"

"There's some open country off the road a piece just shy of town; you oughta make it well before dark. I'll bring some of the boys, and we'll take delivery of these horses there. Figure you could use a break, maybe a drink and a good café meal."

"Bad as my cookin' is, I'd be happy with a poor café meal."

The rider laughed. "I've never met a cowboy yet who could cook worth a damn, me included. The worst end of that deal is that a lot of them become wagon cooks once they've passed their prime, and they never do learn how to cook."

"So that's how that happens," Hewey said in mock surprise. "I can count the number of good wagon cooks I've known on one hand and have fingers left over."

Billy Joe Bradley wasted no time with formalities after they turned the horses over to McKenzie's hands. "Reckon you could part with a dollar or two?" he asked Hewey. "I have a powerful thirst."

Hewey had been calculating the kid's wages— minus one bay mare. True to his nature, he hadn't eaten up to Alvin Lawdermilk's standards, and he found he had saved enough to pay Bradley and be through with him. He counted it off one bill at a time.

"Now you and me are done," Hewey told the young cowboy. "Can't say it's been a pleasure."

"You don't know the half of it," the kid said with a wicked grin, then spurred his horse toward Durango.

I know more than you expect, Hewey thought.

Rutherford, the rider Hewey had met that morning, loped up. "Me and the boys have finished our count," he said, "and you're right on the money, Calloway. I'm headed back, and I'd be pleased to stand you to a drink in town, point you to a good café, and show you the bank. Major McKenzie will meet you there in the morning to settle up."

"I'd appreciate that drink, and could use the pointers."

CHAPTER FOUR

Hewey had his first good meal in weeks, and found he had enough money left to treat himself to a hotel room. He'd just settled into his room when he heard a knock at the door.

"Figured an old lawman like you would find me," he said as Hanley Baker stepped quickly into the room.

"I almost lost you," Baker replied. "I didn't take you for a hotel cowboy."

"Reckoned I'd earned it," Hewey replied. "Don't expect to make a habit of it."

"You got room for two? I'd best not be seen around town."

"You're welcome to the bed," Hewey answered. "Wouldn't want to get too spoiled."

"I've no scruples when it comes to comfort,

because comfort was seldom available in my line of work. Still ain't much of it in my retirement, either, come to think of it. Meanwhile, we've got a plan to hash out before we turn in," Baker said.

Hewey told him about settling up at the bank in the morning, and Baker suggested Hewey camp that first critical evening in the grove where he'd spent the previous night.

"That way I'll know where to find you.

"Stick to the main road gettin' there. It meanders along with the best terrain, so it will take you longer, but there's a lot of comin' and goin'. I don't expect Billy Joe Bradley will try anything out in the open like that; he'll wait for good dark.

"I'll parley with the sheriff while you're conducting your business. Once I've seen your three amateur outlaws leave town, I'll cut across country to be in the grove before they get there. Given a little luck, we can do this without gettin' anybody killed."

"Could you make an exception for that kid?" Hewey asked in jest . . . mostly.

Hewey was at the bank shortly after it opened, carrying his saddlebags over one shoulder. Bryce McKenzie and Trace Rutherford were waiting for him. The rancher made his acquaintance, then led him into the bank president's private office. Rutherford took a seat outside. The tally sheet was already prepared, and the figure comported with Hewey's own number.

"How much of this do you want to take with you, Mr. Calloway?" said banker Oren Jackson.

"Figure I'd better take it all," Hewey answered. "I don't feel comfortable carrying all that money, but I have to see that it gets back to Alvin Lawdermilk."

Jackson smiled. "This day and age, we have safer ways. I can wire it back to Mr. Lawdermilk's bank, and both of us will rest easier."

Hewey thought that over for a minute. It was a new idea for him, but it made a lot more sense than carrying such a sum, especially in light of what he knew awaited him. "I know I'd rest easier."

He fished out Alvin's note to the Midland bank. "Is this all you need to send the money?"

"That will do nicely," Jackson said, "and I'll make out a receipt for the amount you're entrusting to my care. How much would you like in cash?"

"Just what Alvin owes me, plus a little traveling money." He rough-calculated his wages and what he thought he would need for expenses. Jackson had him sign a receipt for the amount he withdrew. The business concluded, Hewey gestured toward a stack of newspapers on a table.

"Reckon I could take whatever you've read? There are folks who expect to see me walk out of here with something in my saddlebags, and I'd hate to disappoint 'em."

Jackson and McKenzie exchanged puzzled looks.

"It's a long story," Hewey said.

After stopping for a quick handshake with Rutherford, Hewey crossed the bank lobby and exited through the double doors in the corner.

He wished then that he'd left Biscuit at the wagonyard so he could saunter down the street afoot for a couple of blocks; he wanted to give his would-be robbers plenty of opportunity to spot him. When he tied the horse, however, Hewey had expected to be carrying real money, and he'd had it in mind to attract as little attention as possible. He decided he'd make the most of the situation and ride slowly with the saddlebags over his shoulder.

Hewey had a medium-sized fire built and was sitting on a log with a cup of coffee in his hand when Billy Joe Bradley stepped into the light, a gun in his hand. His two accomplices entered the camp from a different angle, a few paces from Hewey.

"Had a feelin' I'd see you again," Hewey said.

"You ain't gonna like the reunion," Bradley answered. "I'll take them saddlebags."

"Seein' as how you're holdin' a gun on me, I reckon you will," Hewey said as he passed the amply stuffed pouches.

Bradley smiled broadly as he took possession of what he had waited so long to steal. The two knuckleheads—he remembered their names as Wilkins and

Pinch—crowded in behind him until he waved them back with his pistol. "Don't get greedy," he snarled. "You'll get what's comin' to you soon enough."

"Let's see," Hewey said, his voice sounding surprisingly steady, especially to him. "First he shoots me, and then the two of you. That way he keeps it all, and he don't leave any witnesses. Ain't that about how you had it figured, Bradley?"

"Billy Joe wouldn't double-cross us like that. He wouldn't!" said Wilkins, the tall knucklehead, turning to his partners. "Right?" Clearly, what Hewey had said made him unsure.

"Don't pay him no mind," Bradley answered. "He's just trying to stir you boys up to save his own hide."

"We didn't come here to do no killin'," Pinch chimed in. "We jist wanted to rob Mr. Calloway here."

"And leave him alive to put the finger on you?" Bradley retorted. "You two are even dumber than I thought."

"Maybe we are," Wilkins conceded. "And now I wonder if Mr. Calloway is right and Billy Joe Bradley planned to shoot all three of us." He drew his gun then, training it on Bradley. The other knucklehead followed suit.

Bradley was in a spot, and Hewey sipped his coffee as he watched it play out.

"Now, now," Bradley said, "no need to get all riled up." He was stalling for time, and Hewey imagined that he could see the wheels turning in the kid's head as he scrambled to think of what to say or do. Still holding his own gun, Bradley opened the latch on one saddlebag with his left hand, evidently hoping that the sight of cold, hard cash could distract them.

"Newspaper! Where's the money, Calloway?"

"Sittin' snug in the Midland bank," Hewey answered with his crooked grin. "And now you've got two guns on you and no money. How do you reckon this is gonna play out? Looks to me like you've got your ass in a crack."

"Well, you ain't gonna live to find out," Bradley raged at Hewey, "because I'm gonna kill you right now!"

"Don't reckon you will."

The voice belonged to Hanley Baker, who entered the firelight behind Bradley. Baker had a gun in his hand, too, and his was cocked.

"What in hell are you doin' here?" Bradley was clearly surprised when he turned to see Baker a little more than an arm's length away. "I figured you'd be loungin' around somewhere in your sock feet, restin' your weary bones."

"Looks like I'm here to stop a killin'," Baker replied.

The kid cocked his pistol, but before he had the barrel up, Baker took a quick stride forward with his left foot. As his right foot came to meet it, so did his fist, gun barrel and all. The blow carried the force of most of his weight, and the kid went down like a sack of rocks. His pistol hit the ground in front of Hewey, who quickly snatched it up and leveled it in the direction of the two knuckleheads. They dropped their own guns and stood stock-still.

"How come I never seen you carryin' one of those?" Baker asked him.

"Because I ain't any good with one," Hewey answered. "I couldn't hit an outhouse if I was sittin' over the hole. But then, I never had a good reason to be accurate. Today might be different."

"You got any extra rope in that pack? We might as well deal with these boys right now, before one of 'em takes a notion to escape."

"Oh, my God, you ain't gonna hang us, are you?" came an anguished voice from Pinch. The same one who suddenly had a wet spot in the front of his pants.

"Always carry some spare," Hewey replied.

"Well, tie them two up, if you don't mind, while I hold a gun on the whole crew," said Baker. "Set that one under the tree nearest you," he continued, looking upward at the branches, "and the other one under that one there." He gestured at a tree with a main branch about ten feet high. "We'll drag your dozin' partner to the one over yonder."

"Please, mister, we never done nothin'! It was all just talk," wailed Pinch. Wilkins looked as if he might lose his supper.

"You traveled a long damn way for nothin' but talk," Baker growled. "You had it in mind to rob this man."

"It was all Billy Joe Bradley's doin'! Me and Bert was grousin' pretty hard on the way back to Upton City after Mr. Lawdermilk fired us, talkin' all sorts of crazy talk, when we run into him. He heard us out, then said he had an idea how we could get back at the old man and line our pockets at the same time. The whole thing just growed from there. Next thing we knew we was clean up here, a long way from where we started and smack in the middle of a mess!"

"Well, it's your mess now," Baker said. "Snug your rope around the trunk of that tree, Hewey, and let's get on with this."

Hewey saw what he thought was a wink and a grin when Baker turned toward him. Bert Wilkins finally lost his supper, and Pinch began to moan. "We got laws now, mister," he pleaded. "You can't just hang a man on your own say-so."

Baker glared at him. "I've been a lawman most of my life," he said, "so don't tell me what I can't do. I've put so many ropes around the necks of so many men, I've lost track."

Pinch began to sob, and Wilkins took the dry heaves.

When they had the trio snubbed with their backs against the trees, Baker said, "I wish you'd build that fire up some, Hewey. We got company comin', and I don't want 'em to pass us by in the dark."

Hewey soon heard horses snorting in the distance, and the creak of saddle leather. The men were clearly trying to be quiet, but a couple coughed, and one whispered so loud that Hewey had to chuckle.

"Not exactly professionals, are they?" he asked Baker.

"They're not even good amateurs."

They heard men dismounting, and soon a tall, straight-backed individual with a badge on his chest stepped into the firelight. He looked like a giant to Hewey.

"I kinda expected you a while back, Sheriff," said Hanley Baker as he extended his hand. Will Johnson, the La Plata County sheriff, surveyed the scene as he shook Baker's hand.

"Do you have any idea how hard it is to assemble a decent posse of townfolk?" he said with a disgusted look. "Especially at suppertime?"

"Can't say I've had that dubious pleasure."

"Well, try to avoid it. You get everything from barflies to bankers—eventually. Problem is, you're better off without most of the ones who show up, and the ones you could use are smart enough to stay home. I had to disarm half of these ginks on the way out here to keep 'em from shootin' each other by accident."

He took a long look at the three bound men. Billy Joe Bradley was still trying to collect his wits. "They don't look too vicious," he said by way of appraisal.

"Those two over there are mostly a danger to

themselves, but that groggy one would bear watchin'."

The sheriff took a closer look at Billy Joe Bradley.

"I recognize that one now," he said with a sour expression. "He's been in trouble around here before, but it's been a while."

"That's because he's been in Texas," Baker said.

"I wish he'd stayed there," the sheriff replied.

"We didn't want him," Baker answered.

"Don't blame you," Will Johnson said.

As posse members wrestled them onto their horses, Pinch once again took alarm. "You're a sheriff! Don't let 'em lynch us!"

"What the hell is he talkin' about?" the sheriff asked.

"Damned if I know," Baker answered. Hewey just shrugged.

"Hope one or both of you will come in and sign some papers," the sheriff said.

Baked nodded. "I've got nowhere better to be."

Hewey agreed to come, too.

"You men have someplace to stay? If not, I have a room beside my office with a cot and a washbasin, for those times when the call of duty pulls me away from hearth and home overnight. There's a wood stove in the office, water in a barrel out back, and plenty of Arbuckles' coffee. You're welcome to it."

"I wouldn't know what to do with a proper bed," Hewey said, "but I'd sure spread my roll on the floor."

"It's not a proper bed, just a cot with a thin mattress. Hardly better than what we provide for our guests."

"After all the cold camps and hard ground I've put up with lately, it sounds like the Brown Palace to me," Baker added. "I'll gladly take the cot."

"I've got to tuck these boys in when we get back, so I'll be there for a while. I'll start the paperwork."

"We'll be along behind you," Baker responded. "There should be a little coffee left in that pot of Hewey's, if it hasn't all boiled away. We'll drink that while we snuff the fire. Be a shame to waste it."

The sheriff and his makeshift posse turned back toward town. Hewey could hear Pinch say with relief as the situation began to dawn on him, "Bert, they ain't gonna hang us after all! We're just goin' to jail!"

"Aw shut the hell up!" Bert Wilkins snapped.

Hewey fished Alvin's bottle out of his saddlebag. "My coffee's nothin' to brag about. This'll give it braggin' rights. Did you really hang that many men?"

"A lot of those I brought in went on to hang," Baker answered solemnly. "But that was on the order of a judge and jury. The knucklehead was right about that part; it wasn't my call to make. I've never lynched a man, if that's what you mean. But I also never saw any harm in scarin' the bejeezus out of the likes of these three." His solemn face gave way to a broad grin.

"What do you suppose will happen to them?" Hewey asked.

"There was no hanging offense in tryin' to rob you, but Bradley will do some time," Baker replied. "I've no place to go for a spell, and I'll tell what I saw in court. I suspect those two will bury Bradley pretty deep, tryin' to save their own hides. When it all shakes out, they're liable to get off easy. Any decent jury will decide they're too stupid to have been up to any serious meanness on their own.

"Whatever happens to 'em, it'll be a world better than what Billy Joe Bradley had in mind for 'em— and for you. You had him dead to rights when you warned them about his plans.

"Once he had the money, he would have shot you and them two as well. With no witnesses, he could've gone on his way and nobody would have been the wiser.

"You got some playful in you, by the way, gettin' them three all tangled up with each other, then sittin' back, sippin' coffee, and enjoyin' the show like you didn't have a care in the world."

"Well, I didn't. Did I?"

"Naw," Baker conceded with a grin. "I wasn't gonna let anybody shoot you."

"You did take your time showin' up," Hewey pointed out.

"Jist like you, I was watchin' the show."

"I'd stand you boys to some breakfast, or the county would, anyway," said the sheriff after he joined his guests at the office the next morning. He picked up the coffeepot, and at a nod from Baker, helped himself to a cup.

"Your coffee, your pot, and your water," Baker said. "You're welcome to all you want."

"I'd hate to sponge off the taxpayer," Hewey responded in answer to Johnson's invitation. "I might be one myself someday."

"There's lots of good, God-fearing people in Durango and hereabouts," Johnson countered. "Not everybody, by any means, but there's gettin' to be more every day. After hearing the Word preached, if there's one thing they enjoy it's seeing the wicked brought to justice. You two have provided just such a show, and the courthouse will be packed come trial day. I doubt any of the spectators would begrudge you the cost of a breakfast, and they're the ones pay most of the taxes."

With the delivery complete and the trio of aspiring road agents behind bars, Hewey found himself at loose ends. Alvin Lawdermilk's money was safely deposited in the First National Bank of Midland, so Hewey had no pressing need to return home. As they were finishing breakfast courtesy of La Plata County, Hanley Baker gestured in Hewey's direction with his butter knife.

"What are your plans now, cowboy?" Baker asked after swallowing. "Headed home right away?"

"Thought I might finally enjoy that vacation I've been tryin' to take," Hewey answered. "Hang around here a while."

"Town living can drain a man's bankroll," Baker responded. "The trial won't commence for a couple of weeks, so I'm thinking of doin' a little fishin' in one of the streams that feeds into the Animas River here. There's not hardly time to make it to my cabin and back. That's assumin' the old cabin is still there. Ever been trout fishin'?"

"Most I've ever done is wet a few worms tryin' to snag a catfish. Not a whole lot of runnin' water in West Texas, as I'm sure you know."

"I can recall some times when I nearly perished of thirst in that hard ol' country, but there's plenty of water up here. The time'll pass in a hurry. We can tell tales and swap lies."

"I've been accused of doin' both at the same time," Hewey said with his crooked grin. "Before we go, though, I'd like to enjoy the sights and delights of the big city."

"Better set aside a couple of days," Baker advised, "because Durango isn't one of those places you can see in an hour. It's a city, sure enough. This is my first time back in a while, but even a few years ago there were better than a hundred businesses. The saloon trade was well represented, but there were stores of all kinds, cafés, hotels, and wagonyards.

"Durango even has two railroads. One mostly runs up into the mining district, but it stays busy haulin' men and supplies out and silver ore back to the smelter here."

"Figured I'd check myself in at the nearest wagonyard and enjoy the comforts of a nice cozy stall at night," Hewey said. "Seems a shame to waste money on a hotel where I don't sleep any better than I can in a bed of straw. I'll work out from there durin' the day and see if I can drink Durango dry durin' the evenin's. That'd be a lot better use of my money."

"I've got a little business I can tend to for a few days and meet up with you at the wagonyard at night, though I may be sound asleep by the time you come draggin' in. Once you've had all the fun you can stand, we'll go fishin'."

It didn't take long for Hewey to decide that Hanley Baker was right; Durango wasn't just a town tucked away in the mountains, but a sure-enough city, at least by his lights. Later that day in his meanderings, Hewey also found a different place to eat. The food wasn't as good as it was where the sheriff had fed them, but it was cheaper, and it was a world better than Hewey's own cooking. The price attracted workingmen, including a few other cowboys in town between jobs, so Hewey didn't have to feel self-conscious about his manners.

His evening revelry was a disappointment, however. Hewey discovered that it wasn't all that much fun to drink by himself in a crowd of strangers, something that seldom happened back in familiar territory where he was almost sure to run into a friendly face. And in a rare moment of foresight, he decided that making a fool of himself might undercut his credibility on the witness stand anyway. All in all, he found that the entertainment portion of his vacation fell far short of his usual standards. He was ready to go fishing.

"On our way out of town," Baker said the next morning after they saddled up, "what say you and me make a quick stop at the sheriff's office and see if they've nailed down a trial date? I'd hate for them three to go free because the two star witnesses failed to show up."

"That would be unfortunate," Hewey agreed.

"He what?" Hanley Baker couldn't believe what he'd just heard, and Hewey's eyes were wide open, his mouth uncharacteristically closed tight.

"You heard right," answered Sheriff Johnson. "Billy Joe Bradley made bail."

"How the hell did that happen?" Hewey demanded.

"It was all legal, though I can't rightly believe it was proper," Johnson replied. "News travels fast, and one of the kid's friends showed up to visit him yesterday. Later in the day a local lawyer by the

name of J. Pinkney Dobbs walked in with a bail order signed by the judge, along with a receipt from
the court clerk's office testifying that bail had been
made. I had no choice but to turn him loose."

"Wisht we'd known about it," Baker said, shaking
his head. "We both would have raised sand over it."

"I had no idea where to find you," the sheriff responded, "or I sure would have."

"Whoever put that money up was a fool," Baker
continued. "There ain't a snowball's chance in hell
that Bradley will show up for trial."

"The odds are probably worse than that," Johnson agreed.

Hewey just stood there, too dumbstruck to say
any more. All he could think of was that the law
didn't make any more sense than water running
uphill. That mental image reminded him of something that made infinitely more sense under the circumstances.

"Let's go fishin'," he said to Baker.

"I wouldn't be gone more than about a week,"
Johnson advised. "I talked to the prosecutor after
Bradley walked out of here, and he's pushing for a
speedy trial before we lose the other two."

"I'd say that ain't likely," Baker offered, "but
screwy things seem to happen around here. Nothing against you, Sheriff, but that judge has question-
able judgment."

"He also has a stern temper, and when Billy Joe
Bradley fails to appear in court—as I'm sure he
will—the judge will take it real personal."

The La Plata County courtroom was packed on trial day, just as Sheriff Will Johnson had predicted. And there was a lot of courtroom to pack. Hewey had appeared in a few small-town courtrooms, usually to pay a fine resulting from overexuberant celebrating. Each one was as large and elaborate as the bond issue the county's taxpayers would tolerate, but none held a candle to this one.

Both the prosecutor and Billy Joe Bradley's lawyer, the J. Pinkney Dobbs mentioned by Sheriff Johnson, laid out their positions as the trial commenced. As expected, there was no Billy Joe Bradley.

Fishing is a sedentary pursuit the way Hewey did it, and the long lulls in the action provided plenty of time for daydreaming or thinking. For the last week Hewey had often wondered who paid for the kid's bail and who was paying for the lawyer. Hewey's limited experience with lawyers told him the barrister was not likely to be doing any of this out of the goodness of his heart.

The judge led off. "Counselor," he asked, "where is your client?"

"I wish I knew, Your Honor," the defense attorney replied. Hewey was pretty sure he meant it.

"The court finds Billy Joe Bradley to be a fugitive from justice and hereby orders that his bail be forfeited. We will try the defendant in absentia. He had an obligation and every damned chance to be here."

Hewey grinned his crooked grin. This was starting out to his liking.

In his opening statement, the prosecutor described the robbery attempt as related to him by Hewey and Baker, though Hewey could barely recognize the account for all the lawyerly wording it came wrapped in. Then the kid's attorney laid out his version, a fine fiction in which the two knuckleheads had attempted to rob Hewey, and would have but for the fortunate arrival of Billy Joe Bradley, who bravely stepped in to stop them. Hewey got halfway to his feet with every intention of proclaiming—loudly—that Bradley's lawyer was a baldfaced liar. Hanley Baker grabbed him by the waistband of his britches and pulled him back down before he opened his mouth.

"Don't get overheated, Calloway. It's the man's job to come up with a fairy tale that has just enough of a truthful sound to it to plant what they call 'reasonable doubt' in the minds of a juror or two. He'd tell some other tale if it sounded better. It ain't personal to him."

"Well, it's damn personal to me," Hewey retorted, loudly enough to turn quite a few heads. "That son-of-a-bachelor had his gun pointed straight at me."

"We'll both get the chance to tell what really happened soon enough, but you need to cool down a little bit before then."

Baker was the prosecution's first witness. He related how he came to be in Colorado in the first place, his trailing of the attempted robbers, and their nightly palavers with Billy Joe Bradley.

"And would you please tell the court what you observed on the night in question?"

Baker described the attempted armed robbery, and he included more details than Hewey had noticed at the time.

Then the defense attorney took a run at him. "Mr. . . . Baker, is it?"

"Yes, sir. Hanley Baker."

"You were quite detailed in your recollection, Mr. Baker. Is that because you've had weeks to concoct and practice a story?"

Baker stared him straight in the eye. "No, sir. It's because I've spent the better part of my life wearin' a badge, Texas Rangers, mostly. I taught myself to see and remember details the average man would overlook."

"No further questions, Your Honor." Bradley's lawyer evidently knew when he'd run up against a man he couldn't shake.

The prosecutor stood up again. "Redirect, your Honor?"

At a nod from the judge, the prosecutor approached Baker. "Mr. Baker, for the benefit of the jury, could you elaborate a bit on your law enforcement background?"

"I'm pretty much retired now," Baker began, "but for most of my life I was a Texas Ranger or a local lawman. Went back and forth over time."

"And why was that, Mr. Baker?" the prosecutor asked.

"Because the State of Texas was tight with a dollar," Baker answered, drawing quiet laughter from many of the spectators. "Ranger pay would barely keep a man fed, and then only if he did his own cookin' and had a poor appetite. Like most Rangers, I was lured away several times by better salaries as a sheriff or town marshal. After a time, sittin' still would wear on me, and politikin' never was my callin', so I'd go back into the Rangers and starve a while."

"How many years would you say your law enforcement career lasted?" the prosecutor asked.

"Well," Baker replied, "I'm about fifty now, and I first joined the Rangers after they reorganized in 1876. I'd been up the trail twice and cowboyed some before that, but my lawman career lasted about twenty-five years all told. I quit a couple of years ago when I felt myself slowin' down. Knew too many old boys who didn't take the hint and retired in a pine box. Nowadays I pick up a few jobs as a deputy and that sort of thing."

"And how did you come to be here?"

"It was one of them kinda jobs," Baker said. "I was hired to foller Mr. Calloway up here and see that he didn't get robbed of a sizeable amount of money."

"Thank you, Mr. Baker," the prosecutor said. "The State calls Hewey Calloway."

Hewey settled into the witness chair uncomfortably, what with everyone in the courtroom staring at him. He looked for a place to put his hat; finding none, he began alternately rolling and unrolling the right side of the brim. He rolled it a little tighter when called on for testimony.

"Mr. Calloway, would you tell the court a little about yourself and how you came to be here?"

"I've been a cowboy for about fifteen years, ever since I turned my back on the cotton fields in East Texas and went west. I was hired to deliver a herd of young mares from West Texas to Mr. Bryce McKenzie. It was my poor judgment to pick that Billy Joe Bradley as my helper, and he's been a thorn in my side ever since. I never had any idea he was outlawed . . ."

"Objection!" yelled Bradley's lawyer, Dobbs. "It has not been established that my client is an outlaw!"

"May I remind Your Honor that he's a fugitive from justice?" countered the prosecutor.

"Objection overruled," the judge said. "Continue, Mr. Calloway."

"Well, as I said, I didn't know Bradley was anything worse than a reckless kid with a mean streak. He killed one durned good horse out of meanness and nearly crippled or killed a bunch of 'em by stampedin' the whole bunch over a bridge bein' reckless. It wasn't until pretty far along in the trip that Baker slipped into camp one night to warn me about Bradley's plans to rob me once I'd been paid for the horses."

"Now would you tell the court what happened the night of the attempted robbery?" the prosecutor asked.

Dobbs jumped to his feet with another objection, but sat back down when he saw the judge's scowl.

"I was sittin' by my fire, makin' a pot of coffee, when the kid—Billy Joe Bradley—and those two knuckle . . . citizens he had workin' with him stepped into the light. Bradley had his gun pointed straight at me."

"And what, if anything, did he say?"

"He said, 'I'll take them saddlebags, Calloway.'"

"And then?"

"That's when Hanley Baker showed up and spoiled the robbery."

The defense attorney jumped to his feet. "Objection, Your Honor! That there was a robbery to 'spoil' is purely conjecture on Mr. Calloway's part."

"Overruled," said the judge, sternly. "'I'll take them saddlebags' sounds like a robbery to me."

"But Your Honor, we have only Mr. Calloway's word that my client said that."

"That's why we have trials," the judge retorted, "to let a jury sort fact from fiction."

The defense attorney started to respond but sat down instead, shaking his head.

It looked to Hewey as if the judge was already

running short of patience with lawyer J. Pinkney Dobbs, a development that could and certainly should bode ill for Billy Joe Bradley. If anybody ever caught up with him. After prompting by the prosecutor, he related Baker's pistol-whipping of the kid and their seizure of the two knuckleheads, then the arrival of the sheriff and his posse. He felt pleased with his own testimony and acutely aware that this one story at least lacked his usual elaboration.

Then the kid's lawyer got his crack at Hewey.

"Mr. Holloway . . ."

"Calloway. Hewey Calloway."

"Mr. . . . Calloway," he said, in a manner that implied doubt as to Hewey's real name, not to mention his testimony, "did my client enter the firelight alongside the two individuals you claim to be his accomplices?"

"No, Bradley come at me head-on while the other two were behind me, pretty much."

"'Pretty much'? Were they or were they not behind you?"

"They was sort of off at an angle, but mostly back of me."

"So Mr. Bradley could have been pointing his gun at them, couldn't he?"

"Why would he do that?" Hewey responded. "The three of them were in it together."

"And for that we have only Hanley Baker's testimony, correct, Mr. Calloway? Did anyone else see the three of them together at any time?"

"Lots of people are bound to have seen them leave town together."

"And how many of those imaginary witnesses are in this courtroom to offer such testimony?"

"I am, and I'm not imaginary." The voice came from a tall, thin man who rose out of the audience.

"Me too," said another.

"I saw them." The third volunteer was a stern-faced woman.

Dobbs visibly slumped. "I . . . I have no further questions for this witness, Your Honor."

"You are excused, Mr. Calloway," the judge said.

Hewey thought lawyer Dobbs looked like a whipped dog. All he lacked was a tail to tuck between his legs.

"Your Honor," said the prosecutor, "I recognize the day is still young, but in light of these new developments, I request a recess until tomorrow morning so I can consult with the three volunteer witnesses for the State."

"So granted. Court is adjourned," said the judge as he slammed down his gavel. "I look forward to what they have to say."

"Please tell the court how you came to see Billy Joe Bradley and the two other men involved in the attempted robbery, sir."

"I tend bar," said a ruddy-faced individual with the pallor of a person who spent most of his daylight hours indoors. "I see a lot of people, most of them regulars and the others generally easy to overlook. Those three stood out. They'd picked a table in a corner, and that Bradley was sure telling the others how the cow ate the corn, waving his hands and pointing at first one and then the other. This went on the whole evening. It looked like some kind of fight was going to break out any minute, and rowdiness doesn't make for good business. I look for things like that."

"Thank you. No further questions."

The defense attorney passed on a cross-examination, and the prosecutor called on the tall man who'd spoken up first.

"The three of them almost ran my hack off the road, riding side by side and hurrying as if they had somewhere to be. I was returning to town from a day of business in the outlying area when I rounded a bend and suddenly there they were. They made no attempt to get out of my way so I was forced to get out of theirs. That Bradley looked me right in the eye with a cold expression that made me glad they had just run me off the road instead of robbing me and maybe leaving me dead. He had that sort of a manner to him."

The defense attorney made no effort to cross-examine him either, and Hewey surmised that the three unexpected witnesses were making hash of the defense he had planned.

The stern-faced little woman took the stand next, and explained that the three had watered their horses at her windmill on the edge of town.

"I was sitting on my front porch, knitting in the last good rays of daylight not thirty feet from the water trough when those heathens rode up, watered their horses, and rode on. Not a one of them so much as glanced in my direction, much less gave me a 'Thank you, ma'am' and a tip of the hat for the use of my water. I don't mind folks watering their horses or teams, and I don't charge them for it, but I also don't hold with rudeness, and I fear what this country's coming to with the current crop of young people."

Once again Dobbs had no questions.

Finally, the prosecution brought out the two knuckleheads, one at a time. The sheriff had them locked up as far apart as possible so they couldn't be accused of concocting a story between them, and they were held outside the courtroom so one wouldn't be influenced by the other's testimony. He needn't have bothered; the two saw things pretty much from the same point of view and were mostly interested in heaping the blame for all their miseries on Billy Joe Bradley.

Together they buried him deeper than the defense attorney could dig. Wilkins was the second of the duo to take the stand, and by the time he finished, the attorney's head was drooping. He simply waved off a cross-examination without bothering to say anything.

The prosecutor's closing arguments reviewed the evidence and asked the jury to return a guilty verdict against Billy Joe Bradley. Hewey was happy to hear little lawyer talk to muddle the story. For his part, J. Pinkney Dobbs stuck to his tale of a robbery in progress by the knuckleheads and a courageous intervention by Bradley. Hewey figured that was all he had. After so much testimony to the contrary, people in the audience were rolling their eyes, as were some members of the jury themselves. Hewey was almost embarrassed for the lawyer, though there was a wide stretch of country between "almost" and "embarrassed."

The jury was escorted out of the courtroom but returned after only a few minutes of deliberation. The foreman's "We find the defendant, Billy Joe Bradley, guilty" seemed little more than a formality to Hewey after all the testimony, but it was good to hear it anyway. The judge handed the kid a five-year sentence in the Colorado State Penitentiary, plus another three for failure to appear, and two more for "cause." Hewey decided that "cause" meant the judge was madder than a barn cat in a bathtub.

"I doubt he will emerge a model citizen," the judge told the audience, "but at least he'll be out of everybody's hair for a spell. That's assuming he's caught and returned."

In the interest of saving county taxpayers the cost of two trials and in consideration of their testimony against Bradley, the judge reduced the charges against the knuckleheads to time served. He also attached a proviso that the two leave the Centennial State as fast as they could travel and never set foot on Colorado soil again.

Hewey laughed along with the courtroom audience when Pinch agreed to the involuntary exile. "That won't be hard, Judge," he said earnestly, "'cause I don't have a clue how we got here in the first place."

CHAPTER FIVE

Calloway! Hewey Calloway!"

The voice came from Hewey's right, and he could see someone waving a hat from against the far wall. In between was a whole herd of people streaming from the courtroom toward the open doors. Hewey began to swim across the current.

"Excuse me. Pardon me." Hewey bumped, jostled, excused, and pardoned himself all the way through the throng, then flattened his back against the wall. Once there, he found himself downstream of the hat-waver and had to edge his way against the flow, complete with more excusing and pardoning.

The arm waving the hat belonged to Trace Rutherford, who had taken delivery of Hewey's herd that evening outside Durango. When Hewey finally reached him, Rutherford put his hat back on and extended his hand to shake.

Hewey guessed Rutherford to be about his age, maybe a couple of years older. He was solidly built, though none of it ran to fat. Broad-shouldered and deep chested, he was one of those men who just looked like a natural leader, and Hewey didn't have to be told that he was Bryce McKenzie's foreman.

"Good to see you again, Mr. Calloway, and I sure enjoyed the show," said Rutherford.

"Good to see you, too, and the name's just plain old Hewey. My part of that show didn't come easy. Sweat was breakin' out all over, and I felt like I'd halfway swallowed a big rock. It wouldn't go on down and I couldn't cough it up to chew it, either."

Rutherford laughed with Hewey, not at him. "I could tell you were uncomfortable up there on the witness stand."

"Don't think I've ever had that many people starin' at me before, and I've pulled a few stunts in public. The worst part was tellin' what happened without puttin' a little polish on it. It'll be a whole lot better yarn when I'm not tellin' it under oath."

Hanley Baker had waited until the crowd cleared to cross the corridor and thus avoided all the excusing and pardoning. "Hanley Baker," he said as he extended his hand.

"Nice to meet you, Mr. Baker. The name's Rutherford, Trace Rutherford."

"Hewey told me about meeting you and your

boys. Coulda picked you out of a crowd. Conversation runs thin between two ol' boys in a week of futile fishing, and I've pretty much heard his whole life's story without having to draw a word of it out of him."

"I'm just natcherly friendly," Hewey said.

"Natcherly windy, too," Baker jested.

"I'd like to hear some of those windies," Rutherford said. "The café down the street brews a good pot of coffee."

"Where's the nearest saloon?" Hewey countered. "After all that testifying, I'd sooner have a cool beer or two, and I'll stand the first round."

Hewey's recommendation won out over the café and coffee.

"Well, now that the trial is over," Rutherford said to Hewey and Baker, "what do you boys plan to do with yourselves?"

"I figure I'll provision my cabin, squat there for a while and enjoy the scenery, then pull up the drawbridge and hunker down for winter," Baker answered. "Staples are cheaper now than they'll be in a couple of months when everybody else gets around to buyin' at the last minute."

Hewey took a long sip of his beer, then conceded to having no firm plans.

"You're welcome to come join me," Baker offered. "It's a long way back to West Texas."

"I appreciate it," Hewey replied, "and I may show

up after it's all said and done, but right now there's still a lot of new country to see, and this looks like a good jumpin'-off place."

Rutherford pondered that briefly, then turned to Hewey. "It's a little late in the year to be jumping off too far," he said, "but I can show you quite a bit of new country right around here."

He waved his arm slightly as if to draw Baker into the conversation, and continued. "We're about to start bringing horses down from their high summer range, and I could use a couple of extra hands, if you two are interested. The pay's decent and our wagon cook can dish out a pretty good meal as long as nobody sours his mood. The regular hands go out of their way to avoid that."

"I'll compliment him on every bite," Hewey chuckled.

"I'll fluff his bedroll if that's what it takes," Baker chimed in.

"Sounds like you're both in," Rutherford said. "Happy to have you aboard."

"The wagon and the remuda went on ahead before I left to watch the trial," Rutherford told Hewey and Baker as they approached the Slash M headquarters. "It's mostly uphill, and hard on the wagon team, so we always allow for short hauls and frequent rest. It's also better if the saddle horses don't start out tired.

"A couple of boys went along to help where

they're needed, and we'll go up with the rest of the crew if they haven't already given up on me and started on their own. I didn't figure on the trial taking two days. But this job is pretty much the same from one year to the next, so they don't really need me until a question comes up."

"I've been meaning to ask how you got loose to watch that show, what with the work comin' up and all," said Hewey.

"It was an unexpected pleasure," Rutherford explained. "Major had planned to go himself, but other business pulled him away, and he sent me instead. He'll want a full briefing when we get back, and it might be good if you boys joined us; I could forget some detail or other and need to call on one of you."

"Oh, Good Lord, don't call on Hewey!" Baker snorted. "Won't any of us recognize the story once he's had time to add his 'polish' to it."

Rutherford was quick to laugh, a trait Hewey appreciated. He'd spent more time than he cared to around men with no sense of humor.

A young cowboy stepped out of the bunkhouse wearing his longhandles, a shirt and hat, and his right boot. The other foot sported a lumpy-looking cast almost to the knee.

"Welcome back, sir!" he hollered to Rutherford. "Everybody left yesterday, and I sure wish I could have been with 'em."

Rutherford shook his head in mock exasperation. "Speedy Martin, I keep telling you, you don't 'sir' a sergeant. You can 'mister' me if you want to, but save the 'sirs' for the Major."

"Yes, sir . . . I mean, Mr. Rutherford."

"Hell, to everybody else I'm Trace or Rutherford," the ranch foreman said to Hewey and Baker after they'd ridden past, "but ol' Speedy insists on being formal. He's just a kid and not long from home, so his manners are still fresh. It won't take the other boys long to corrupt him."

"What happened to his leg?" Baker asked.

"Bronc smashed it into a post in the round pen, played hell with his ankle. I hope it will heal okay after my crude doctoring. He's a good kid and a natural cowboy, and I hate to see him start so young collecting the battle scars that plague those in our line of work."

As the trio detoured to the corrals to unsaddle, Rutherford reined up, twisted around, and hollered at the young puncher. "Speedy, how many saddle horses did the boys leave behind?"

"I'd say a half dozen or so," the kid replied.

"Good," Rutherford said. "We'll need three, and I hate to leave the headquarters short in case something comes up."

"Won't be anybody here but me and Major McKenzie, once he gets back," Speedy pointed out, "and unless I can learn to mount from the off side, I won't need a horse. I'd never get this cast in the near-side stirrup."

"I'll bet you could figure it out."

"Yes, si— Mr. Rutherford."

"And you need to get some pants on," Rutherford joshed. "What if womenfolk were to show up here?"

Speedy took the comment seriously. "Lordy, do you think they might? I'd hate to cut the leg off my only pair of pants, and otherwise I could never get this cast through 'em."

"Remind me and I'll find you a pair from my barracks bag. Can't have a Slash M hand going around in his underwear."

"No . . . Mr. Rutherford."

Hewey had quite a few of the battle scars Rutherford had mentioned, and he was ready to change the subject before he started tallying them. "Several times I've heard you call your boss 'the Major,' and just now you said something about bein' a sergeant. What's the story behind that?"

"I served under Major McKenzie in the cavalry," Rutherford replied. "Would've followed him anywhere. He wasn't the sort to raise his voice or lose his temper, but he expected his orders to be followed, and right smartly. Those who didn't do so were gone pretty quick. Nobody got the usual Army bawling out, but the Major could be awfully firm, and once he'd made up his mind, there was no turning away from a decision. I never saw him make a bad one, and that inspires a lot of confidence among the men under an officer, me especially.

"I never made it past top sergeant myself, but I finagled around until I got appointed to his small staff of officers and noncoms, and I stuck to him like glue. Couldn't have pried me loose with a claw-hammer."

"Where'd you serve?" Hewey asked.

"We got in on a touch of the Apache campaign and then patrolled the Border during one of Mexico's revolutions. Then we got pulled off and shipped to California when the ruckus started with the Spaniards. Ended up in a place I'd never even heard of before then, clear across the ocean, a place called the Philippines. If you're looking for new country, that was sure enough new country to me."

"So was Cuba. I was there with Colonel Teddy's bunch."

"As I recall," Rutherford said with feigned annoyance, "you boys got most of the headlines."

"Yeah, I suppose we did. That was Colonel Teddy's doin'. He was as good at politickin' as he was at soldierin'. Maybe better," Hewey said with a grin. "Our part didn't last all that long, and I missed a good bit of the scrappin' laid up in a field hospital."

"Wounded?"

"No," Hewey said, shaking his head, "the officers warned us to boil the water before we put it in our canteens, but I've drank out of muddy hoofprints, so I didn't pay 'em much mind.

"I'd have been a lot better off," he continued with a wry smile, "if I hadn't been so damned smart."

"It's too late in the day to get started up the mountain," Rutherford commented after they finished at the corrals and walked the short distance to the bunkhouse, "so we'll stay here for the night and saddle up by lantern light in the morning. You'll leave your horses here to lounge away the next couple or three weeks. A man works for Major McKenzie, he goes mounted on a Slash M horse. They're all mountain raised and know how to take care of themselves in rough country. We've lost very few of them."

"That's comfortin'," Hewey said with a slight wince. "It'd be even more of a comfort if you hadn't lost a one."

"He's never caught short for words, is he?" Rutherford said to Baker.

"Not once since I've known him," Baker agreed, "though he come close up on that witness stand."

"You can't be serious!" Rutherford said, his eyes widening in surprise. "I've heard of people doing that, but never figured I'd meet one."

"Oh, we did it all right," Hewey insisted. "Me and ol' Snort Yarnell treed the whole crowd in that saloon. Them broncs were pitchin' for all they were worth. It was legs and hooves goin' everwhere, and both horses slippin' and slidin' on that slick plank floor. The only safe place in that gin mill was behind the bar. Several fellers were cut off and shinnied out a couple of windows, and a few went out the front door.

"Next thing I saw was Snort's pony runnin' near

head-on into the big center pole that held up the tent roof, and down she come! Never realized how heavy that much canvas could be until it fell on my head and squashed me down even with my saddle horn."

Rutherford was laughing so hard tears ran down his cheeks.

"H-how did you get out of that jackpot?" Rutherford asked, the question interrupted several times by his own laughter.

"I don't think me and Snort could have found our way out from under that dark canvas if the horses hadn't done it for us. They saw daylight from the front door and made for it like a drownin' man grabbin' at a rope. They quit pitchin' much then, with all that weight bearin' down on 'em, which I appreciated, seein' as I was between the horse and the weight."

Rutherford by that time was doubled over, one hand on his belly and the other bracing himself on his saddle horn. He was breathing hard and gasping.

"The only problem was that they both hit the door at the same time, and it was barely wide enough for one horse and rider; noways would it do for two. Snort's pony must have found some footing then because he squirted out ahead of mine. Ol' Snort was wallowin' off on the near side, hangin' on by his right spur where he'd hooked it under his off side stirrup leather. Once he was out in the open, Snort's bronc set in to pitchin' again, and it sure was a comical sight.

"Right about then I saw the top of that door-way comin' at me fast, and all of a sudden I had too much survivin' to do to pay any more mind to Snort. I had to duck down so low that I ended up hangin' off to the side too, and my horse went to pitchin' again just like Snort's. It was a show that people woulda paid good money to see, but I didn't hear any cheerin', just a bunch of ol' soreheads cussin' up a blue streak.

"We never were welcome in that establishment again."

The conversations ran from one topic to another, from the merits of various horse lineages—everyone had their own opinions—to discussions out of the blue.

"Either of you ever heard of baseball?" Rutherford asked during a lull in the conversation. "It's all the rage up here. There are teams in most towns, and even some at the mines. The newspapers are full of it, though I can't make heads nor tails of what they're saying. It's all about 'batters' and 'catchers' and 'pitchers.' And what the heck is a 'fielder'?"

"I seen a game once in Fort Worth," Hewey answered. "I'd ridden up there on the T&P"—the Texas and Pacific Railway—"to nursemaid a carload of C. C. Tarpley's best sorry bulls to the Fort Worth Stockyards. There was a game that night, for the same price as a glass of whisky. I probably would have been better off with the whisky. I finally figgered out a little of what was goin' on, but first I had to get past the sight of grown men in knickers."

Baker and Rutherford both got a kick out of that.

"So, what's a 'fielder'?" Rutherford asked.

"I think that's what they called the boys away out in the pasture. They didn't have a lot to do, as best I could tell, and they spent most of their time flirtin' with the single women up in the stands. It was decent entertainment, but I'd druther have seen a circus. Or a ropin'."

Hewey and Baker were paired up on the mountain. It was one of McKenzie's rules; his cowboys worked the higher country in pairs at least. The terrain was rough and the rocks were slick when they stayed put. A sizeable share of them refused even to stay put and insisted on slipping and sliding at the worst possible times. McKenzie didn't want an injured hand lying up there waiting two or three days to be discovered and patched up. Or buried.

Hewey found Baker to be a better than competent cowboy. His bad leg didn't slow him down on horseback, and despite having several years on Hewey, his eyes were still sharp; he caught the slightest hint of movement, sometimes before Hewey himself did.

"You get sensitive to that kind of thing in my line of work, or you don't live very long," Baker explained when Hewey remarked upon it. "Sometimes all you see is a quick flash of a white shirt or glint off of a spur. If you miss it, you might not get a second chance."

They found the horses in small groups. Horses are herd animals and seldom like to be completely alone. In that respect they were a lot like people, Hewey had decided long ago. He had wintered alone in a few New Mexico mountain line cabins, making rounds when the snow wasn't too deep, dragging cattle out of drifts or making sure they stayed where they belonged. The work was fine, and usually fairly easy. He didn't even mind the cold too much, though he had noticed in recent years that the winters were colder than they used to be, and they caused more misery for his hands, feet, and joints.

What Hewey objected to was months passing with no one to talk to. So he talked to himself for fear that he might otherwise forget how. He was even reduced to arguing with himself sometimes, though the disagreements seldom lasted long because he usually found himself to have been right in the first place.

Like the other teams, Hewey and Baker would gradually gather the scattered horses from their sector into something like a small herd during the day and push them down toward lower ground by late afternoon, the various small groups coming together before nightfall.

It was during that late-afternoon push a few days into the gather that Hewey asked a question he first thought of a couple of hours before, when he and Baker were several hundred yards apart, well out of talking range.

"In your Ranger years, did you ever run into a feller by the name of Len Tanner? He wore the same badge."

"Len Tanner? You bet," Baker answered. "We mostly worked different districts, but things tend to muddy up when you have outlaws on the move, which is most of the time. Ol' Len and I partnered up on several hunts. How come you to know Len Tanner?"

"Me and my brother Walter were in his custody for a day or so once," Hewey said.

Baker turned and stared at Hewey, waiting for the joke. When it didn't come, he said, "I can't wait to hear that story. Spill it."

"Me and Walter were new to West Texas, two overgrown kids from the Blacklands and green as gourds on the vine. We didn't know sic 'em from come here about cow country etiquette, that you're supposed to howdy a camp before jist ridin' in. We was also starved down with nary a penny between us and no place to buy food if we'd had anything to buy it with. I even thought about eatin' one of our horses and doublin' up on the other. Lean as we both were, it wouldn't have been much of a burden."

"So where does Len Tanner fit into this story?" Baker asked.

"It was his camp we rode into just as bold as you please. Damn near got ourselves shot for it, but ended up gettin' fed instead. The next day we run onto a couple of ol' boys pushin' a herd of cows and calves south at a pretty good clip. They took us on for six bits a day and some fast-fried beef. Them two didn't even take time to cook biscuits."

"I think I'm beginnin' to see the picture. . . ."

"I didn't know squat about beef cows," Hewey continued, "but even I could tell they was pushin' them cows too hard; the babies couldn't hardly keep up. When I said somethin' about it, the one in charge told me he was payin' me to herd cows, not to give advice. Directly more riders showed up, spurrin' hard and comin' on. The two fellers we were workin' for quit the herd and flushed like quail, leavin' me and Walter with a herd of cows that turned out to belong to C. C. Tarpley."

"That doesn't sound too promisin'," Baker said.

"It was downright spooky," Hewey said. "C.C. and some of his boys took us in tow while several of his hands went on after the other two. Back at C.C.'s miserly headquarters, he locked us up in an old dugout. That's where we were when Len Tanner showed up with the cow thieves. It was ol' Len who puzzled it all out. The next day he escorted all four of us to the judge at Upton City. Len sort of semi-vouched for us and we told our story to the judge, earnin' us—me, mostly—the undyin' enmity of the two thieves.

"That was our introduction to West Texas, and Len Tanner was a part of it from the beginnin'."

"Sounds about right," Baker observed, "and I can't tell that you dolled it up much."

"I would have," Hewey said, "but I didn't figger I had time to do it up right. We'll be at the wagon in an hour or so."

Baker just smiled and shook his head.

"Say," Hewey added, "was ol' Len a big talker when you was with him?"

"Biggest talker I ever knew," Baker answered, "until I met you. Len would talk until my ears bled, but he was rock-solid when he needed to be. He was with me when I took that bullet in my leg."

"I'm gonna guess it wasn't him put it there."

"No, he was the one who took it out. He covered me until the fugitives we were chasin' took off. Then he dug that slug out with his old-timey fightin' knife. I've never had anything hurt that bad since. He let it bleed long enough to flush all the poisonin' out, then cauterized it with his knife. It left me a little gimpy, but ol' Len saved my life.

"Once he got me to civilization, he went on after the men we'd been chasin'. A week or so later, he brought 'em in, both tied across their saddles and dead as last year's grass. Len was of the old school and didn't have a lot of patience with formalities."

"I guess he'd mellowed a little by the time me and Walter met him," Hewey said.

"Don't count on it." Baker laughed.

❖

The noon meal was a two-man affair of leftover biscuits and beef from breakfast; it made no sense for the hands to be going to and from the wagon at midday, especially since the trip would be down and back up. Breakfast and supper were thus the cook's busy periods.

About a week into the gather the wagon and the growing herd of horses had made it to lower ground. One evening as the tired hands were gathering for supper, Hewey spotted a rider approaching. Baker saw him, too, as did Rutherford, who walked off a ways from camp to greet the new arrival. Even from a distance Hewey sensed who he was. He was in civilian clothes, but nevertheless, Hewey fought back a momentary urge to salute him.

One of the Slash M cowboys went out to take charge of the man's horse, and Rutherford shook hands with his boss before escorting him on into camp. "Major," Rutherford said, "I'd like you to meet Hanley Baker and Hewey Calloway. Boys, this is Major McKenzie."

"Mr. Calloway and I met at the bank when I formally took ownership of those young mares," McKenzie said, shaking hands with both Hewey and Baker.

"I had forgotten that," Rutherford said. "A lot has happened since then."

Rutherford, McKenzie, Hewey, and Baker sat on bedrolls and a jutting rock as Rutherford accurately detailed the court case, including the bail-jumping by Billy Joe Bradley. He called on Baker to fill in some background, and even tapped Hewey for a bit of color. Hewey tried to tell the story straight, but he diverged ever so slightly from a factual narrative a time or two.

"Major," Baker said, "I hope you'll pardon Mr. Calloway here. He means well, but he has a somewhat enlarged fairy-tale gland."

McKenzie never lost his military countenance, but still managed to smile approvingly. "I thought I detected something of the sort," he said.

"Trace, I appreciate your report, and the assistance of Misters Baker and Calloway. I had every intention of watching the trial myself, but business does not always conform to a man's preset schedule. I had the opportunity to negotiate the sale of several carloads of horses to the Army next year," McKenzie explained, mostly to Hewey and Baker, for Trace Rutherford already knew the nature of his trip, "and one does not turn down a chance to grasp the proverbial bird in the hand."

"It was my pleasure to watch it for you, Major," said Rutherford. "I don't suppose you heard anything in your travels that might give this crew something new to talk about? We've all rehashed the trial story to the point where we've about talked it to death."

McKenzie thought for a few seconds before answering. "There was one thing. A trio of young bandits robbed the express office at Trammell Junction.

Two of them shot and killed the clerk in the process. The story I heard in Durango said the clerk did nothing but explain that he didn't have the combination to the safe; he was killed for telling the truth. The manager of the office opened the safe after that, and he was the source of the account making the rounds. The few people who saw the bandits leave all agreed that they rode south toward New Mexico."

"You don't suppose . . . ?" Hewey said to Baker.

"Wouldn't surprise me a bit," Baker replied.

Rutherford caught their drift. "You're thinking the three included that Billy Joe Bradley and the friend who visited him in jail just before he was sprung."

"Like I said," Baker answered, "it wouldn't surprise me."

At supper McKenzie and Rutherford entertained Hewey, Baker, and several of the Slash M cowboys with stories from their cavalry days. The remaining hands had heard the stories before and busied themselves with other subjects.

The cavalry stories continued at breakfast the next morning before the wrangler brought the remuda together and the crew began roping out their mounts for the day. They were all saddling up when Baker noticed a rider approaching at a slow lope, awkwardly.

"We've got company!" he hollered, and both

Hewey and Rutherford joined him to watch the approaching rider.

"That looks like Speedy," Rutherford said, walking out a ways in that direction.

The rider reined up a respectful distance short of the camp, observing proper etiquette despite what appeared to be considerable excitement.

"Mr. Rutherford, sir, I need to see the Major!" Speedy reported breathlessly.

McKenzie quickly set his plate down and walked out to the young puncher. "What's happened, Speedy?"

"Major, sir, we've been robbed!" Speedy replied.

"Robbed? What do you mean?"

"At just barely daylight this morning, I heard a commotion at the corrals and stepped out the bunkhouse door to see what it was. Three men, the youngest one about my age and the other two not much older, had brought the horses in from the trap and were busy roping out new mounts. I knew they weren't any of our outfit, so I hollered, asking what the hell they were doing. Pardon my language, sir. That youngest-looking one took a shot at me and I ducked back inside. He and another one fired two more times at the door. If I'd had a gun I would have shot back, but I didn't have so much as an old squirrel rifle."

"Be glad you didn't, Speedy," McKenzie reassured him. "At three against one, you wouldn't have stood a chance."

"Well anyway, sir, they hightailed it out of there

on three of our horses. The ones they come in on was jaded and worn down. I'm sorry I couldn't stop 'em, Major. I saddled up and finally wrassled myself aboard. Been coming as fast as this horse could take it. Again, I'm sorry, sir."

"You did fine," McKenzie told him, in a manner that made it clear why the man's cavalry troopers and now these men were loyal to him.

"Major," said Baker, "I have a strong feeling that the three express office robbers and your three horse thieves are the same bunch, and I think Hewey and I know the youngest one, by the name of Billy Joe Bradley."

Hewey nodded his agreement.

"I don't take horse theft lightly," said McKenzie, "and I won't have one of my men shot at. Speedy, come back with me, and I will go on to Durango for the law."

"With all respect, Major," said Baker, "by the time you got to Durango and brought the law back with you, those fugitives would be long past the county line, maybe the next one or two as well. All a town posse could do would be to scatter sign and then go home. This is the sort of thing I've done most all of my life, and I'm passable good at it. Me and Hewey can go on as private citizens and foller 'em all the way to Canada if we have to."

"We can?" Hewey interjected, but Baker continued.

"We'd just appreciate the loan of a couple of fresh horses once we get back to the headquarters."

"We would?" Hewey tried again. And again, no one paid any attention to him.

McKenzie paused, clearly running Baker's plan through his mind. It took him only seconds to decide. "Your idea has merit, Mr. Baker, but you won't have to run those men to ground without any backing; you will go on with the support of the Slash M. A crime was committed on my property and I won't stand for that.

"Speedy," McKenzie said, "are there still two fresh horses at headquarters?"

"Yes, sir," the young puncher answered.

"Then we'll leave here as soon as you and Mr. Calloway are ready," McKenzie told Baker. "Go get you something to eat, Speedy, then come on down at your leisure. It must be hard to ride with that cast on."

"It is, sir," Speedy replied.

McKenzie then turned to Rutherford. "Will we be leaving you shorthanded, Trace?"

"No, sir," Rutherford said. "We're far enough along that we can finish up in a few days with the men who'll still be here."

"Then that is how it will be."

Hewey's assessment of Bryce McKenzie's leadership kept improving—but now he wasn't so sure about Baker.

"What in the world are you thinkin', draggin' me along on this manhunt? I told you I'm no good with a gun," Hewey said to Baker as they finished sad-dling.

"You're fine with your carbine, aren't you?" It was more of a statement than a question.

"I can keep myself fed."

"Some of the best Rangers I knew almost never drew a six-shooter. They'd rather use a rifle or a shotgun."

"I still don't think I'm the best man you could have picked for this deal."

"Remember what I said about Len Tanner, Hewey? He was a big talker and slow to anger, but he was rock-solid when need be. I saw how you handled that run-in with Bradley and the two knuckleheads. It was three against two, and you were solid. Well, it's gonna be three against two again when we catch up with those boys. I made my choice, and I'm pretty sure I picked the right man."

Rutherford saw them all off, carrying a flour sack tied closed with twine. "Cookie sent you the leftover biscuits," he said. "Some of the boys donated the second ones they'd planned to eat at noon. Said you two would likely need them more than they would."

"Thank 'em for us, would you?" Hewey said be-fore tying the sack to his saddle horn.

"Good luck," Rutherford said solemnly.

"Aside from more biscuits," McKenzie said, "I can provision you back at headquarters."

"We won't need much," Baker informed him. "We'll be traveling fast, light, and probably damned lean. Cold camps and uncooked meals, mostly. Beef won't keep long, and I ain't one for raw meat."

"Then you're in luck," countered McKenzie as they rode away from camp. "We have a smokehouse half full of hams, a variety of sizes. They will keep well, so take whatever you wish."

"Major, we're going to need rope to truss them boys up when we run 'em to ground." Baker was trying to anticipate what would be necessary, but Hewey could tell he was a little rusty.

"I can supply all you need," McKenzie said, "and do better than that." He stepped into his house for a few moments and emerged with three sets of shackles. "They're obsolete, but thoroughly secure. We used them on some renegade bandits on the wrong side of the border. I kept them as mementos of my service with the cavalry."

"I appreciate the loan, and will try to bring 'em back in good shape," Baker told him.

"Godspeed to you," McKenzie said. "I will notify the authorities in Durango while you're gone."

"I been givin' that some thought," Baker replied. "We got our suspicions, and I think they're good ones, but right now all we're after for sure is three horse thieves. As big as this county is, and what with Durango and the mines and all, I'm of the opinion that horse thievery is kinda low on the totem pole to the sheriff's office anymore. Why don't you let Hewey and me see what we're dealin' with before callin' on the law? They might could spare a deputy in a week or so to come ask a few questions, but they're probably stretched pretty thin."

"No crying wolf, then?" McKenzie said, more statement than question.

"No sir, so far just a few coyotes," Baker agreed.

CHAPTER SIX

Hewey and Baker rode out of the Slash M headquarters compound by late afternoon, a little more than eighteen hours behind the outlaws. The sun was well down in its arc, but that helped Baker pick up the fleeing horse tracks, as they cast deeper shadows in the slanting light.

"They didn't try to hide their trail," Baker said to Hewey. "That'll probably change as they get what they think is a good lead on any pursuit. It'll also slow 'em down. We'll keep on 'em until it gets too late to see, then pull off and try to grab a little shut-eye until the moon comes up. It'll be full and probably cast enough light to see by. Sleep will be even sketchier than mealtime on this trip, so I'd recommend taking what you can get."

"I'm happy to say that you're the boss on this

foray." Hewey grinned. "And I'm jist the hired hand. I like that a lot better than I did the previous arrangement."

They picked a grassy spot and hobbled their horses, then swapped the bridles for halters so the horses could graze. In the interest of time, they loosened their cinches but didn't unsaddle. They were mounted again and on the move as soon as the moon rose, then stayed horseback all night, Baker stepping down periodically to reassure himself that they were still on the trail. A couple of hours after good light, Hewey caught sight of fresh wood where a branch had been broken off a pine tree that overhung the tracks. "Broken-off branch back yonder," he said to Baker, whose attention was mostly on the ground.

"I have a hunch what that may mean," Baker answered, "and there it is." He pointed out to Hewey where the tracks were blurred out ahead of them.

"Looks kinda amateur to me," Hewey opined.

"It is," Baker agreed, "but it shows they've started thinking about hiding their trail. And that they're traveling slower. This is all to our good."

Before long they encountered the broken-off limb, tossed to the side but not hidden. "These boys are sure careless," Baker said.

"Let's hope they stay that way."

After a few miles Hewey and Baker came to a stream and let the horses water out. The tracks went into the water, but Hewey didn't think he saw where they came back out on the opposite bank. Baker raised his hand for Hewey to wait, then waded his horse into the stream, crossing to the opposite bank but not exiting. He stood up in his stirrups to get a better look, then called Hewey to follow him.

"Wait on the other side there if you will, Hewey, while I find where they came out."

He turned downstream without hesitation, scanning the far bank as his horse plodded slowly with the current. Slick creek rocks caused the horse to slip a couple of times, but he never went down; Rutherford had been right about the sure-footedness of the mountain-raised Slash M mounts. About a hundred yards downstream Hewey saw Baker emerge from the water and wave for Hewey to join him. Once there, Hewey could see the tracks leading onward.

"You seemed to know where you were going," he said to Baker. "How did you figger out which way they went?"

"The logical thing to do would be to head upstream," Baker explained, "especially when the stream cuts the trail at an angle, like it does here; upstream slants in the overall direction they're headed. Nine times out of ten your average fugitive will figger that out and go the other way to throw off pursuit, believin' they're the only ones who ever thought of it."

Hewey shook his head in mild wonderment.

There was a lot to learn about the lawman business, and a student could do worse than Hanley Baker as a teacher. That's assuming he wanted to learn such a business, Hewey thought.

"Notice anything missin' from this picture?" Baker asked a few hours later.

"Like what?" Hewey answered.

"Like manure," Baker replied.

"Come to think of it," Hewey said, "I haven't seen any in quite a while."

"That's because those horses don't have anything left in 'em to make manure," Baker pointed out. "They're gonna run out of steam before long and leave those boys afoot if somethin' doesn't change."

The sun was getting low when Hewey smelled smoke. Baker was sniffing the air, too.

"You don't suppose those fugitives have stopped to build a fire, do you?" Hewey asked.

"Can't hardly be their fire," Baker said. "They still have a long lead on us, and I can't see 'em stoppin' for half a day or so to lounge around."

It wasn't long before they found the source of the smoke: the chimney of a cabin set in a sizeable clearing, along with a barn, a small set of pens, and various outbuildings. Things were reasonably well maintained, so the place was in regular use.

Hewey and Baker approached the cabin, Baker in the lead. "Hello the house!" he shouted.

A face appeared at one side of the window and shortly the door opened. Out stepped a stocky man of middle age, leveling a shotgun at them. Both hammers were back, and the man did not look friendly.

"You two had best ride on," the man growled, "and catch up to your partners. There'll be no more horse thievin' here." He swung the shotgun north, the direction they were headed, then brought it back to bear on Hewey and Baker. Hewey thought it was centered on him in particular, but then he was a little sensitive to having guns aimed in his general direction.

"We're followin' them boys, all right," Baker said, "but not to join up with 'em. They robbed an express office a ways south of here and killed the clerk, but we're after 'em mainly because they stole horses off the Slash M."

The man with the shotgun appeared to be thinking that over, but the gun never wavered. "Are you lawmen?" he asked. "Don't see any badges."

"I used to wear a badge," Baker replied, "Texas Rangers, mostly, but I retired from that line of work, or thought I did. We ride for the Slash M now."

"There's three Slash M horses in the pens yonder, eatin' expensive feed, but I'm reluctant to turn loose of 'em until I get my horses back."

"Figgered you might be," Baker replied. "So I'm offerin' a deal. If you'll take these two in trade for a couple more of yours, we'll bring all five home to you in a few days and swap out. No stealin', just borrowin'."

Again the man appeared to think it over. Slowly he lowered his shotgun and said, "Come on in the house and have some coffee. I can fix somethin' to eat directly." Then the man shook his head. "Don't know why I'm trustin' you, but I am."

"It's just my honest, friendly face," Hewey said with his usual grin. He felt he'd been left out of the conversation so far, an intolerable state of affairs.

"We can't take the time to eat," Baker said to Hewey's disappointment, "but we sure could use the coffee. Haven't stopped anywhere long enough to brew any."

"You boys look lank, so I'm gonna insist that you eat," the rancher said with a tone of finality, "or the deal's off. Go swap your gear onto the gray and the dun yonder, the only horses I have up right now. You'd best watch that dun. They're both steady horses, but the dun is a little playful at first. I'll have some venison ready to eat by the time you get back. Won't be as good as if I'd floured it, but it'll be nourishin'."

Hewey saw nothing wrong with the offer, and Baker reluctantly agreed. "We're sure obliged to you, Mister . . ."

"Samuels," the rancher replied, "R. T. Samuels. Most people around here call me Artie."

"My name's Hanley Baker, and my partner here is Hewey Calloway. Don't get him started tellin' stories, or we'll never get out of your hair."

Hewey just grinned his crooked grin.

Hewey took the dun, and Samuels was right; the horse humped up as soon as he swung the saddle on. He drew the cinch tighter than he normally would, both to be sure the saddle would stay put and to squeeze the dun so that he would be winded more quickly once he started to pitch.

They wolfed down the venison, but lingered long enough for a second cup of coffee each. Hewey thought the food and the coffee were excellent, and he complimented Samuels on both as he and Baker mounted up. "You were just gaunt and thirsty," Samuels replied. "When you come back through here, we'll do it up right."

"Our horses were about used up when we got here," Baker said, and Hewey thought he could see a plan forming in the ex-Ranger's head. "Do you have any neighbors about as far north of here as the Slash M is to the south? That's where them renegades are liable to remount themselves next, and we should, too."

Samuels had already been thinking along those lines, Hewey reasoned, because his answer came almost before Baker finished. "There's a lot of folks scattered to the north, but the most likely to have their horses snatched, given the distance, would be a young couple, the Hendersons. I sure hope them fugitives don't hurt either of 'em, the little lady in particular, if you know what I mean."

"I'm inclined to doubt it," Baker said, "because those boys may still feel too pressed to take the time. I hope so, anyway."

"Well, good luck to you," Samuels said as Hewey and Baker left at a slow lope, "and watch that dun!"

Hewey kept waiting for the hump in the dun's back to snap and the horse to break in two. It was always a little unnerving when a horse threatened mischief but dragged the suspense out until just the wrong moment. After about a mile of that he lost patience and suddenly jabbed the dun's ribs with his spurs. The startled horse responded with a pitching fit that threatened to unseat Hewey a couple of times.

"Stay with him, Calloway!" Baker yelled. "We can't spare the time for me to chase him all the way back to the Samuels place!"

Hewey found the horse to be clever with his lunges, hard four-footed landings, and repertoire of sudden spins and reversals, just not as clever as the bay mare he matched wits with months earlier. He was lifted off the seat of the saddle a few times but never lost a stirrup.

Unable to dislodge its rider, the dun soon tired of the game and settled down. There was no longer a hump in his back. Hewey wished his own back could loosen up as quickly.

Nightfall found them repeating the grazing, rest-ing, and remounting routine. Hewey welcomed the chance to close his eyes, and fretted at his inabil-ity to sleep. The fretting must have been a dream, however, for the next thing he knew, Baker was shaking him awake.

"You sure do sleep hard," Baker said. "Liked to've never got a response out of you. Moon's well up, and we need to be back after it."

Hewey was groggy much of the remainder of the night and was grateful that the dun stayed settled. He marveled at Baker's ability to read signs in the moonlight. Hewey considered himself pretty good at tracking, as most of the better cowboys were, but he drew the line when the sun set, moon or no moon. Within a couple of hours after daylight Baker reined up. Judging by the jumble of tracks, it was apparent that the outlaws had stopped and milled around.

"Looks like they had themselves a parley here," Baker said. "We can expect somethin' squirrelly be-fore long."

Within a half mile the tracks split and went three ways. "They look to be tryin' the old Comanche trick of scatterin' like quail and then pullin' back together later," Baker said, "after they'd confused whoever might be comin' on behind 'em. Three quail also don't make much of a covey. I'm goin' to take a wild guess and say these boys will come back together away up yonder where the mountain juts out."

"I'm beginning to trust your hunches," Hewey replied, "but that's easier when I know what they're based on. Why there?"

"It's the only real landmark around that sticks up high enough to show over the trees," Baker told him.

"What if they've divided up their loot and gone their separate ways?" Hewey asked.

"Gone where?" Baker countered. "With the mountains on both sides, they're hemmed up in this valley. No, they'll come together."

Hewey couldn't argue with Baker's logic. "So which hooligan do we follow?" he asked.

"Right up the middle," Baker said. "It's gonna be the shortest route; the other two would put more miles on these horses just to circle around and get to where this middle track is goin', and I'm countin' on takin' advantage of their two tired horses. It will slow all three of 'em down."

"I'm sure glad that you're the ramrod and I'm just the wrangler," Hewey said with a tired grin.

About midday Hewey and Baker reined up at another stream. "We'll water out here," Baker said as he dismounted. Hewey could see that Baker's bad leg was bothering him; he limped more than usual, and once Hewey saw him simply stop before moving on.

"Which way this time?" he asked. "Upstream or down?"

"We might as well flip a coin," Baker replied. "Could be either one, but it don't matter. We're goin' straight on."

Hewey cocked his head at an angle, quizzing the older man without putting the question into words. "We know where he's goin', so we'll strike his trail directly," Baker said.

In less than a mile Hewey saw tracks angling in from the east. "Downstream it was."

It was late afternoon when they neared the jutting finger of mountain. Within a mile, another set of tracks joined the ones they had been following. Another half mile and the third set of prints came in sight. Baker said nothing but kept on the now-wider trail. It curved around the outcrop, nearing the river before once again swinging in the direction of the mountains. It then met and merged with a dim set of wagon ruts running north and south; the outlaw trio had more or less paralleled it all the way, Hewey thought.

"How far do you reckon we've come since the Samuels place?" Hewey wondered aloud.

"Pretty near as far as it was from there back to the Slash M headquarters," Baker replied. "We need to keep our eyes open for the Henderson homestead." His expression was grim, and it was clear to Hewey what he was thinking.

The tracks they'd been following took a quick bend to the west, along with an even dimmer set of wagon ruts. Those ruts led to a house and out-buildings in a clearing.

As they approached, a gunshot rang out, and from the sound of the report, Hewey could tell it was aimed in their direction. Baker lifted the reins in his left hand and raised his empty right hand to shoulder level, palm outward, and Hewey followed his lead. They both reined up.

"We mean no one harm unless you're the three outlaws we've been tracking for days," Baker said loudly.

"You could have done without that last part," Hewey said quietly. "What if it is them boys?"

"It's not," Baker said, and Hewey followed his gaze toward a lean-to next to the barn. A young woman with a rifle stood against the wagon sheltered there. Her dress was bloody and her face looked grim. She held the rifle as if she meant to use it.

"Ma'am," Baker said loudly, "we mean you no harm."

"Why should I believe you?" the woman said, still holding the rifle on them.

"Because it's clear even from here that you need help," Baker said.

The woman lowered the rifle then, though she still held it. "My husband needs more help than I do," she said, her head bent and her eyes downcast. "He's shot up pretty bad."

Baker rode in closer and Hewey followed suit. "What can we do?" Baker asked.

"There's an older couple a few miles south, a white man and a Mexican healing woman. Her people call her a curandera, and folks around swear by her. I was fixing to hitch the wagon team up and take Nate to her."

"I don't see no team," Hewey said. It was really a question rather than a statement.

"Those savages ran them off, along with the spare horses. They're out that direction." She pointed toward the mountains.

"I'll go get 'em," Hewey said, "and bring the wagon along to the house once they're harnessed."

Baker nodded approval, then said, "I'd like to see your husband, ma'am. I'm no doctor, but I used to be a lawman, and I've dealt with more than my share of gunshot wounds, some of 'em my own."

Mrs. Henderson led him to the house, where her husband lay on the porch. He was unconscious and crudely bandaged with strips of white cloth, the bandages soaked with blood in a few spots.

"I've stopped most of the bleeding," Hewey heard her tell Baker, "but these wounds here won't quit seeping through."

"You done real well, ma'am. I'll help you with those bad ones" were the last words from Baker that Hewey could hear before he was out of earshot in the horse pasture. The grass was curing that time of year, but there was still plenty of green to interest horses. Hewey found a dozen head just over a nearby rise, circled behind them at an easy trot, then began moving them toward the barn and open pens. Among them he spotted two more heavily built draft animals and three ridden-down saddle horses carrying Samuels's brand. The others appeared fresh.

Hewey swung the team and wagon around as close to the house as he could, set the brake firmly, and stepped down. Circling to the back of the wagon, he pulled the pins and removed the tailgate, carrying it to the porch.

"We can move him on this," he said to Baker, and to Mrs. Henderson he added, "I laid out the saddle blankets from the barn for your husband to lie on, and when I unsaddle my horse, you can have my blanket to sit on. I figger you'll want to ride in the bed and tend to Mr. Henderson."

"Hewey, you've read my mind," Baker said. "We've been in an all-fired hurry to catch them renegades for the killin' they've done so far, but we can't help that express clerk now. Best we can do is prevent this man from dyin' and addin' another black mark. You can't hang a man twice.

"You take Mrs. Henderson to the curandera and I'll go on ahead to track 'em as far as I can. Probably be gone a couple of days, then I'll come back and get you."

"Don't tangle with them boys alone, Hanley. Three against two is dicey odds, and three against one is liable to be suicide," Hewey cautioned.

"I'm touched by your concern," Baker joshed, "but don't you worry about that. I'm old, and I didn't get that way by bein' reckless. A big part of a lawman's job is just follerin, keepin' his eyes open and his butt in the bushes. I've done this a few score times before." Then he grinned. "Didn't realize you was so anxious to tangle with 'em."

"I'm sure no gunslinger," Hewey agreed, "but we've come this far, and I'd hate not to see it through."

Night caught Hewey and the Hendersons on the trail south, a fresh Henderson horse tied to the wagon and Hewey's gear in the bed. The full moon that had provided light for Hewey and Baker in the beginning of their journey had started to wane, but Hewey could still see landmarks such as the jutting rock as well as gaps in the trees that presumably led to houses.

"If you see anything that looks familiar, Mrs. Henderson, holler out. Hardly notice trace chains among all the other noises in the daytime, but they sure make a clatter in the quiet of the night. How's Mr. Henderson doin'?"

He was talking as much to keep himself and the woman awake as he was for any other reason. He hadn't slept more than a few hours total over several days, and she had been through an ordeal that sapped all the energy from her. Hewey knew she needed rest even more than he did, but he could never find their destination without her help.

"I can't see his wounds in the dark," Mrs. Henderson answered wearily, "but I've heard him moan a few times, and I think he's fevering."

She directed Hewey off the trail a couple of times into empty meadows that necessitated turning around, and each time she apologized.

"It's not your fault, ma'am," Hewey assured her. "We'll find the right road directly."

In another hour she tapped him on the back, startling him awake. He hadn't realized he'd been driving in his sleep. "This is it, I'm sure of it," she said.

Hewey reined the team to the right, into another gap in the trees. He could dimly see another clearing ahead and thought he smelled smoke from a near-dead fire.

"Ma'am," he said, "what do I call these folks? I don't know a name."

"They're the Swensons," she answered. "I think he's from Sweden or one of those countries."

"I've heard of it," Hewey said. "He's probably right at home amongst these mountains, trees, and cold winters."

As they drew near the cabin, Hewey yelled out, "Hello the house! We've got a badly wounded man out here! And a woman who could use some tendin' to as well!"

He saw a flash of light in a window and then the increasing glow of a coal oil lamp. The lamp moved into another room, and soon was joined by light from a lantern. The door opened and a gray-haired man in overalls stepped out barefoot with the lantern, struggling to slip his free hand through the remaining strap of his suspenders. A small woman with graying black hair followed close behind, throwing a shawl around her shoulders. She took the lantern from the man and moved quickly to the wagon. There she looked first at the man lying in the bed, then at the woman. Hewey had a strange feeling that she could see the whole story in those two brief glimpses.

"Quickly," she said in heavily accented English, pointing toward the house and adding, "La casa."

Hewey and Swenson carried the wounded man into the house, and at the woman's direction, placed him on the bed. The dark-skinned little woman put an arm around Mrs. Henderson and shooed Hewey and Swenson out the door. They retired to the porch, where Hewey filled the man in on the story as best he knew it. The older man merely shook his head, mumbling to himself at intervals.

"My wife has a gift," he finally told Hewey. "If he can be saved, she will do it."

Swenson's English was as heavily accented in its own way as his wife's was in hers, but it struck Hewey that there was nothing lacking in his thinking.

❖

After unhitching the Henderson team and turning them loose in the Swensons' pens, Hewey suddenly felt the strain of the last several days weighing on him and moved to the wagon to wrap himself in his blanket. The nights had been getting cooler, which helped him stay awake on those long rides but chilled him a bit once he got still and quiet. He thought how much better he would feel in his bedroll, which was still on the Slash M wagon. It would be many more cold nights before he would see it again, and by then he might no longer need a bedroll. He struggled to push that thought aside so he could sleep.

The sun was well up in the sky by the time Hewey's eyes opened. It hadn't been that many hours, but it was the longest stretch of sleep he'd had in more days than he could say for sure. It left him groggy and a little confused. Was this the Samuels place, the Henderson place? No, he recalled, he was at the Swenson place, and he had no idea how the Hendersons were doing.

Hewey folded his saddle blanket and moved to the porch. He was suddenly aware that he smelled like a horse. That was probably an improvement, he decided. Shortly after Hewey sat down, Swenson emerged with a cup of coffee.

"My Maria thought you could use this," he said, then sat down on the edge of the porch with his own cup.

"How are they doin', the Hendersons?"

"Maria says Mr. Henderson will survive his wounds, but it will take some time. With her herbs she brought down his fever; that's what kills so many."

"And Mrs. Henderson?" Hewey asked.

"She is a strong young woman," Swenson replied.

"I don't know how long I can stay," Hewey said reluctantly. "My friend went on from the Henderson place to track them outlaws alone, and I really need to join up with him before too long. If I don't, I'm afraid he may wade into 'em alone."

"Is your friend a foolish man?" Swenson asked.

"Not a bit," Hewey told him, "but he's an old lawman with a powerful sense of the right and wrong of things. He was already dead set on bringin' those three renegades to justice, and after what they did to the Hendersons, he rode on with blood in his eye."

"Then you should go today," Swenson said.

"I was kinda figurin' to take the Hendersons home," Hewey countered.

"That won't be for many days, too many for you to stay," Swenson told him.

"But how will they get home?"

"When it is time, we will take them. Maria is not for riding a horse, but she is good with driving our buckboard. I will drive the Henderson wagon and Maria our buckboard. We will come home that way."

"I'd sure like to pay you for your trouble," Hewey said. "I have more money in my pocket than I'm used to, and I'll just spend it on tomfoolery once I get the chance. It's a habit of mine."

"Maria will accept no payment, Mister . . . I don't know your name."

"No, I don't recall that we actually met," Hewey said. "My name is Hewey Calloway and my law-man friend is Hanley Baker. In all the excitement, I reckon we forgot the formalities." He extended his hand to shake.

"I am Lars Swenson, Mr. Calloway. Maria says her gift comes from God, and to accept pay for it would dishonor Him."

"Can't argue with that," Hewey said. "I thank you for your hospitality, Mr. Swenson, and you're right, I probably should be goin' back."

Hewey caught and bridled the Henderson saddle horse, then led him to the wagon to saddle him. As he finished, Mrs. Henderson stepped out onto the porch.

"I don't know how I can thank you enough for all you've done for us, Mr. Calloway," she said. "Nate would be dead now if it weren't for you."

"You just get well . . . both of you," Hewey said awkwardly.

"I was thinking the strangest thought just now," Mrs. Henderson replied, "how times like these can change a person's priorities. Nate surprised me last year with a set of bedsheets, a luxury we really couldn't afford. He said it might make our little homestead feel more civilized to me. I loved those sheets, and now they're mostly gone, torn into strips to make bandages. The bedsheets were a luxury, but the bandages were a necessity. I can sleep on blankets, and thanks to the Swensons and the two of you, I won't have to sleep alone.

"You be safe, Mr. Calloway, you and Mr. Baker as well."

"Yes, ma'am." Hewey stepped up into the stirrup and swung his right leg over the cantle of his saddle. He tipped his hat to her and was off at a slow but ground-eating lope.

Baker was nowhere to be seen when Hewey rode up to the Henderson place late that evening, so he unsaddled the horse and turned it out in the pens. A man never set himself afoot deliberately when he was in sparsely settled country like this, so he never gave any thought to turning the horse out. Instead, he poured out a bait of oats and forked some hay, then refilled the wooden water trough from the hand-pumped well.

He built a fire in the Hendersons' small cast-iron stove and put a pot of coffee on to boil. The coffee was just boiling when he heard hoofbeats outside. *A fine amateur lawman I am*, he thought.

My carbine is in the barn with my saddle. When he looked warily out one window, he saw it was Baker.

"Hello the house!" Baker said.

Hewey stepped out the door. "How's coffee sound?"

"Pretty damn good right about now," a tired-looking Baker answered.

They emptied the pot as they talked out on the porch, watching the light fade.

"First off, how are the Hendersons?" Baker asked.

"That Mrs. Swenson seems able to work miracles," Hewey replied. "Mr. Henderson should come out of this in one piece. Mrs. Henderson is still worried half to death, but she'll come out of that as he gets better."

"As long as they're in good hands," Baker said, "I feel better about things."

"So what did you find out?" Hewey asked.

"That we may have had a stroke of luck. I trailed 'em for about a day until they pulled up at a wide spot in the road—not a town, not a settlement, only a ramshackle general store and saloon. I hung back and watched 'em leave. They didn't go far, just a little ways, and set theirselves up a camp of sorts back in the trees by a little meadow. There they staked their horses out to graze and rest. Them boys are vicious but they're not stupid. The only way to go from there was up, and the horses they stole from here wouldn't make it if they was to push on without rest and somethin' to eat."

"Neither will we," Hewey ventured. "I was about to borry a little bacon off the Hendersons, and there's a chicken coop added on to the back of the house. Found half a dozen eggs that will be spoilt by the time they get back. Neither one of us can make biscuits so's you'd recognize 'em, so bacon and eggs is what it will be."

"Could as well be Delmonico's. We can grab a few hours of shut-eye after we fill our bellies, then leave before first light. I think we'll catch up to those renegades before dark tomorrow."

After they ate and washed the dishes they'd used, Hewey and Baker walked to the barn for their saddle blankets. Recalling how helpless he'd felt when he heard Baker ride up, Hewey drew his saddle gun from its scabbard.

"What do you shoot in that thing?" Baker asked.

"Forty-five," Hewey answered. "Figured I could always find ammunition for such a common round."

"Have any extra?" Baker asked.

"Nearly a whole box," Hewey replied. "You runnin' short?"

"No," Baker told Hewey, "but I've got somethin' you might need before this is all over." He dug into his off-side saddlebag and pulled out an oily rag, unwrapped it, and thrust a well-worn Colt at Hewey, grip end first. "It ain't much for looks anymore, but it's still tight, smooth, and accurate."

"I already told you I can't hit nothin' with one of them," Hewey objected.

"Sometimes affairs like the one we're about to get into happen at a range so short that a man's accuracy ain't all that critical. This ol' thumb-buster won't do anybody any good in my saddlebag, and it might just save your life. Or mine. I wisht you'd hang onto it."

Hewey reached into his own saddlebag and withdrew the battered box of cartridges. He pulled the hammer of the pistol to the half-cock notch and flipped the loading gate open, loaded one round, skipped the next chamber, then loaded four more before fully cocking the hammer and letting it down on the empty chamber. It was a common way to load a Colt, and the only truly safe way to carry one. Seeing as how Hewey planned to carry it in the front waistband of his britches, he wanted it as safe as possible; he might like to have an heir or two someday.

"I've been about half afraid to ask," Baker said, "but Mrs. Henderson, did them boys . . . ?"

"No," Hewey answered. "I'm sure they would have if they'd had the chance, but from what I could piece together, when her husband went down, Mrs. Henderson stepped right out onto that porch, gathered up his rifle, and stood 'em off until they gave up and rode on."

Baker let a smile cross his face, and it looked to Hewey as if he visibly relaxed.

"I guess I should've told you sooner," Hewey said. "It was a relief to me when I heard it, and it never dawned on me that you were still worryin' over it."

"Don't matter," Baker answered. "I know now, and it's lifted a big ol' black cloud. If they'd done what I was afraid they'd done, I might've shot all three of 'em without givin' 'em a chance to surrender. It would've been wrong, but I'd have done it."

"I'd have helped you," Hewey said.

A few hours later, Baker brewed another small pot of coffee while Hewey brought the fresh horses in under the fading light of the moon, and they drank the coffee as they saddled up. They were well along by good daylight. It was a new trail to Hewey, but Baker had now been up and back, so there was no need to dawdle.

"I wonder, do you have any idea where on this earth we are?" Hewey asked after a couple of hours. "Not that it really matters, I'm jist curious. Might help to know when I tell this tale later."

"Your guess is as good as mine," Baker answered. "I know my own little part of Colorado, and this ain't it. Maybe we'll ask somebody."

"That wide spot in the road up yonder," Hewey continued, "does it have a name?"

"Not that I could see. I didn't dare show myself, so it's not like I could ask anybody, and there weren't any signs or like that. Even the one buildin' didn't have a name on its sign."

"Oh, well, I'll just make somethin' up, I guess," Hewey told him.

"Would it be the first time?"

"You bet. I'm a strictly honest man." Hewey said it with a straight face, but he couldn't hold it long.

CHAPTER SEVEN

Sunset comes early in the mountains, Hewey mused, especially when you're far below the peaks. The end of the daylight was approaching, and so too was the end of the trail, at least as far as Hewey and Baker were concerned. At length, Baker raised his free hand.

"That store is just ahead beyond this bend," he said. "I'll slip up yonder and take a look."

Baker rode up the slope and disappeared into the trees. He was back shortly.

"Those boys must think they're goin' to waltz out of this thing without anybody catchin' up to 'em; the three Henderson horses are tied at the hitch rail in front of the store. I don't want to get some innocent person killed, on the off chance there is one, so we'll wait until daylight and catch 'em in their camp, maybe even asleep. They're sure not goin' anywhere else with dark comin' on."

He led Hewey to a level spot with a good patch of grass and with a screen of trees to conceal them.

"We'll pass the night here, let the horses graze a little, and take turns dozin'. You can have first watch."

That suited Hewey, because he wasn't sure he could sleep anyway. Throughout the trailing and helping the Hendersons, Hewey hadn't given much thought to what might happen once he and Baker caught up with the outlaw trio. It was still in the future, assuming they caught up at all, and Hewey had much more pressing matters on which to focus. Now a confrontation was imminent, and Hewey's imagination was running away with him.

He passed his entire watch with all sorts of dire possibilities running through his mind, but eventually his eyes got heavy, and he had to fight off sleep. When he judged it about midnight by the passage of the moon, he awakened Baker. He first reached to shake the aging lawman's shoulder but stopped abruptly when he realized that it might get him shot or at least clubbed with Baker's gun barrel.

"Baker," he said quietly, "it's about midnight. Baker . . ."

"I heard you the first time," Baker growled, throwing off his blanket and getting stiffly to his feet. "Best sleep while you can," he said. "I'll be wakin' you up soon enough."

Hewey wrapped up in his own blanket and lay

there, still thinking of tomorrow's possibilities. As tired as he was, he was sure he couldn't sleep.

"Calloway," Baker said loudly, "we've gotta go."

Hewey was groggy, but got to his feet and folded his saddle blanket. Baker's horse was already saddled.

"I did a little reconnoiterin' while you were asleep. Them three are still camped where they were, and the cocky SOBs even have a fire goin'. I noticed they never unsaddled their horses last night, though. Probably figurin' on gettin' an early start before their luck runs out. If we get there soon enough, I intend to run it plumb out and catch 'em unawares."

Baker led the way back down to the road, then told Hewey, "We go at a walk as we get close to that store, and we go quiet. Once we get close to the camp we'll tie the horses and go in afoot. Keep a little distance so they can't miss one of us and hit the other by accident. Once it starts, go with your gut and trust your instincts."

"I'm not sure my instincts have been educated up to this," Hewey replied.

At that point Baker reined up and went on at a walk. They passed by the darkened building without raising anybody as best Hewey could tell. About a quarter of a mile farther on, Baker turned off the road and began threading his way through the trees. Another fifty yards or so and Baker raised his hand to stop. He dismounted and Hewey followed suit, both of them tying their reins to low-hanging limbs. Baker motioned for more spacing and then pointed out the direction to the camp.

When he could spy the camp, Hewey saw the three outlaws squatted on their haunches and finishing a cup of coffee each. Their horses were tied maybe twenty paces away.

"Put your damn hands up!" Baker barked.

Billy Joe Bradley and another of the three reached for their guns before Baker fired a shot into the fire, scattering sparks over them. Then their hands went up. The third sprinted toward his horse, ducking behind a boulder about halfway there. He dashed from the protection of the rock, jerked the slipknot in his reins, and swung up into the saddle without taking the time to find the stirrup. Baker fired high just before the young outlaw disappeared into the forest.

"Couldn't afford to lose the horse," he said to Hewey by way of explanation. "We're going to need them all. Now, if you don't mind bringin' our horses up, we'll get on with this."

Hewey was soon back with the horses as Baker held the captured duo at gunpoint.

"Reach in my saddlebags and get a couple of sets of those shackles, then bring up some rope," Baker said.

They shackled the outlaws' hands in front of them, tied them securely back-to-back, and for good measure snugged them to a tree trunk.

"Sure don't want to lose these two birds in the

hand," Baker grinned, then swung into the saddle to follow the escapee. "Be back in a day or so, latest," Baker said. "That jaybird is most likely to try climbin' out, but keep your eyes open and your carbine handy in case he does somethin' different. Meanwhile, if either of 'em gives you any trouble, shoot him.

"On second thought," he added, "shoot 'em both." Then he disappeared into the forest.

It was late afternoon when Hewey thought he heard the sound of shod hooves on rock. He waited for more, but they didn't come, so he decided he'd been hearing things. He didn't imagine the gunshot or the bullet whistling past his head, however, and dove behind the dead tree trunk he'd been sitting on. He saw the runaway outlaw sprint back behind the boulder he'd used as cover that morning.

"Didn't think I'd run out on you boys, did you?" the returnee yelled to Billy Joe Bradley and the other outlaw.

Hewey thought it odd that the tied duo didn't seem all that excited about the potential rescue. He didn't have long to ponder that, however, because the returnee fired another round, splintering the log just above his head. After a couple of seconds Hewey took a deep breath and raised his head, bringing his carbine's sights to bear on the boulder. He fired when he saw a head begin to emerge, sending the young outlaw's hat flying.

Too soon, he thought. Next time he'd wait for a better chance at the gunman's head. That didn't take long, but Hewey's round took a chip out of the rock. *At least I'm keepin' his head down so's he can't shoot at me*, Hewey thought. That didn't last long, as the kid behind the boulder began shooting back. Every time the outlaw's head began to show, Hewey fired, and he usually received a round in return. Once the outlaw tried the other side of the boulder, but Hewey had been expecting that at some point, and swung his barrel quickly enough to keep the kid's gun out of the action. This went on for a minute or two, Hewey firing and the outlaw ducking and firing back. Twice or three times— Hewey wasn't keeping careful count—the outlaw stopped to reload.

Hewey worked the lever of his Winchester again and squeezed the trigger as his adversary peered around the boulder another time. All he heard was a loud click. He tried again with the same result. The young outlaw rose from behind the boulder and advanced on him with the same hateful smirk that Hewey had seen so many times over the last several months from Billy Joe Bradley. The outlaw's six-gun was cocked and his finger was on the trigger. Hewey stared into the muzzle.

The outlaw was no more than a dozen feet away when Hewey heard the sound of a horse crashing through the trees. The young outlaw heard it too, and turned his head in the direction of the noise. Hewey made the most of that distraction, drawing the belly gun, taking rough aim, and thumbing back the hammer. The two loud clicks caught the outlaw's attention, and as he jerked his head back around, Hewey squeezed the trigger. The 250-grain lead slug caught the man in the center of the chest, the impact knocking him backward a half step and triggering his pistol to fire harmlessly into the tree-tops. His eyes registered surprise and shock in the instant before he crumpled to the ground.

Baker suddenly burst from the trees, bareheaded and looking for a target, his pistol drawn and cocked. It took him only seconds to assess the scene, and he slid the horse to a stop. He looked at the six-gun, then back at Hewey's face, nodded his head slightly, and grinned.

"I thank you for the borry of the pistol," Hewey said, his voice a little unsteady.

"Keep it," Baker replied, still grinning. "Might come in handy someday. And now that you have things under control here, I've gotta go back amongst them trees and find my hat while there's still light to see by."

Hewey and Baker unsaddled the five horses and staked them out to graze for the night. Then they carried the outlaw's body away from the fire and left it near the deceased's shackled and tied friends. A reminder—and a warning, Hewey thought. Almost as an afterthought, Hewey covered the dead one with his saddle blanket and took blankets to the other two; it was up to them to figure out how to cover themselves against the night's chill.

"It'd be a lot warmer if we had the bedrolls off our saddles," said the young outlaw with sandy-colored hair. Hewey hadn't bothered to learn the names of Bradley's companions because he doubted either one was using the name he was given at birth. And anyway, one of them was dead already.

"I'll be damned if a prisoner is goin' to sleep better than me," was all Baker said.

Hewey felt the same way, but Baker beat him to it. It didn't dawn on him at the time how unnatural it might seem to let someone else do the talking.

Baker made a pot of coffee, while Hewey sliced off several strips of bacon. The prisoners got what was left over when they were through. Hewey took the first watch, his thoughts troubled over the day's events.

Breakfast the next morning was coffee. It sat uneasily in Hewey's empty stomach, and tossing and turning during Baker's watch had left him groggy and short of sleep. Hewey had been in a pickle or two before, but other than the Cuba foray he'd never shot at a man. Even then he wasn't sure in all the confusion that he'd ever killed anyone. It was hard to put that shoot-out aside, and he knew it would come back to him over and over, like a bad horse wreck, only worse.

At first light, Hewey and Baker saddled their horses, then untied the prisoners.

"Saddle up, all three horses," Baker ordered.

"How are we supposed to do that with these irons on our wrists?" the sandy-haired one asked.

"Figger it out," Baker growled.

Bradley and his remaining partner had difficulty with their own saddles, but found that teamwork, even if clumsy, made it a little easier to saddle the dead outlaw's horse. Hewey wondered if they would make use of that newfound knowledge the next time.

"Now wrap your former partner in one of your tarps and load him aboard," was Baker's next command.

"How do . . ." Sandy-Hair started to ask, before Baker's scowl stopped him.

As they struggled with the outlaw's body, Sandy-Hair exclaimed, "Hey, he's getting stiff! He ain't gonna bend over the saddle!"

"Then you two better balance him real good," Baker answered, "and tie him fore and aft."

"His arms won't turn," Sandy-Hair protested.

"Tie that end by the neck," Baker ordered. "He ain't gonna choke to death."

They didn't bridle the outlaws' three horses but left them haltered as they had been when they were staked out to graze. Hewey tied the shackled hands of Bradley and the other prisoner securely to the

forks of their saddles while Baker watched for any
sign of trouble. His unholstered pistol rested com-
fortably in his right hand.

Baker led Sandy-Hair's horse while Hewey took
Bradley's. The remaining mount fell in behind, following his herd-mates. The outlaw's body stuck out
awkwardly, like a load of lumber tied crossways.
Both of the other prisoners turned to look at him
periodically, and Hewey saw the sandy-haired one
shiver slightly. He thought it would do them good to
see the body swaying to one side and then the other
as the horse plodded along. They stopped at the first
small stream to water the horses, then picked their
way through the trees to the faint wagon road on
more level ground. That route took them past the
ramshackle store, where Baker reined up.

"Hewey, we looked to be runnin' shy of coffee
this mornin', and another slab of bacon wouldn't
be an extravagance. Reckon you could dicker with
whoever runs that outfit yonder? I'll stay with these
boys and see that they don't get lonesome."

After tying his horse and that of the sandy-haired
prisoner, Hewey climbed the two rickety steps to
the porch, walking gingerly across the warped and
crumbling floorboards. It took several knocks on
the door to rouse the proprietor, a tall, thin man
who looked as if he'd sworn off shaving when Colorado achieved statehood. His red-rimmed eyes lit
up when he saw he had customers, but the glow
dimmed when he realized two of them were re-
strained, and his gaze lingered on the tarp-wrapped

body tied so casually across the saddle of the free horse.

"Lawmen, are you?" he asked Hewey. Not waiting for an answer, he continued, "I ain't doin' anything illegal up here, so the law is always welcome."

Hewey thought the smile seemed forced, but not being a lawman, he didn't much care. "We could use some coffee," he said, "and a slab of bacon if you've got it."

The thin man produced two pounds of Arbuckles' coffee and some bacon that Hewey judged edible for a few more days at most.

"I don't get many customers these days since the prospectors gave up on this area," the storekeeper told him. "Sometimes I won't sell a thing for days. Times ain't what they used to be, and maybe they never was. Anything else I can get you?"

"That's all I stopped for," Hewey replied, then paused for a moment. "I don't suppose you have a set of bedsheets for sale."

The shopkeeper tilted his head downward a little and a bit sideways, as if trying to decide whether or not Hewey was serious.

"Bedsheets," he said. "I can't recall anybody ever askin' for bedsheets before. But this modern world is full of changes and surprises. They tell me a couple of boys back east even built themselves a flying machine, so I guess a lawman sleepin' in bedsheets on the trail isn't all that far-fetched." Still, he kept his head cocked a bit.

"They ain't for me," Hewey assured him. "It's a

long story, but a woman back down the valley had to tear hers up for bandages on account of those cutthroats out yonder, and it just come to me that she might be tickled to get some new ones. It was a crazy thought . . ." His voice trailed off at that point. "How much do I owe you?"

"Well, let's see here . . ." the shopkeeper began. Then he chuckled. "You really want bedsheets?"

"I might as well have asked for a slice of green cheese off the moon, huh?"

"Not really," the thin man said, rubbing his bushy beard and clearly pondering something. It looked to Hewey as if he might be trying to call up a long-buried memory. "Hang on a minute." He disappeared through a door into the back of the store. In a few minutes he returned with what looked to Hewey like a bundle of dust.

"I was married once," the storekeeper said. "It was a good twenty-five years ago and it didn't last long enough to count, hardly. Things were booming hereabouts, or we thought they would be. I brought her up from the settlements, and anything she asked for, she got. Then she ran off with a smooth-talking prospector. It wasn't a big loss, she couldn't cook worth a damn anyway.

"It didn't dawn on me until you asked, and even then I had to think on it, but a nice set of white sheets was one of the things she wanted. She was gone before that load of freight ever got here, and they've been stuck away in a cubbyhole ever since, just waitin' for you to show up."

The shopkeeper jotted some figures on a scrap of paper, then announced, "I figger ten dollars ought to cover your bill of goods."

"Ten dollars?" Hewey's eyes got wide. "I ain't buyin' the whole store, just a little coffee, a slab of bacon, and some sheets."

"I figure the groceries at five dollars and the sheets for another five, but if you think you can get it cheaper somewhere else around here . . ."

"No, I reckon I'm stuck," Hewey conceded, "but it ain't hard to see why you don't have many customers."

The shopkeeper beamed as Hewey counted out the bills. "You come back, now," he said.

"Could you at least wrap them sheets in some fresh paper?" Hewey asked. "This stuff is fallin' apart."

The shopkeeper drew some slightly newer paper off a large roll, pulled the sheets out of their crumbling wrap, and repackaged them. Hewey was happy to see that the sheets themselves looked little the worse for their decades of storage.

"Here you go, and no charge for the gift wrapping."

Hewey turned to leave, then turned back to the storekeeper. "Those boys out yonder," he said. "Their horses were tied up out front a night or two back."

"Sure were," the storekeeper answered, "but I didn't know they were wanted. They seemed like a civilized bunch, and happy, too. Spent nearly twenty dollars at the bar. Best night of business I've had in a long time."

"While they were bein' all happy and free-spendin'," Hewey said, "I don't suppose you heard any names."

"Well, sir, I mind my own business and don't eaves-drop on my customers, but I did catch a few moni-kers scattered around. One of those a-horseback out yonder the others called Billy Joe."

"And the other two?" Hewey asked.

"The other one out front was . . ." He gazed off across the room. "One of 'em called him Clay and the other one always called him Hawkins. It was that Billy Joe fella who called him Hawkins."

"And the one under the tarp?" Hewey prodded.

"That Billy Joe called him Sloan, and the other one called him . . . Jesse it was."

"Thanks," Hewey said. "That might be helpful somewhere down the line."

"Always glad to do my part for the law," the storekeeper said. Hewey wasn't entirely convinced, but then he didn't entirely care, not even close.

"What's in the bundle?" Baker asked when Hewey emerged from the store.

"It's sort of a gift for the Hendersons," Hewey re-plied, "Mrs. Henderson, mostly. She had to rip up her bed linens for bandages, and they'd meant a lot to her. You know how women can be partial to nice things. I thought it might help her feelin's to have some new ones."

Baker gave him a long appraising look, then chuckled. "Who the hell else would think of such a thing, and especially at a place like this?"

"I got the last ones," Hewey said with a grin.

Baker set a deliberate pace on the return trip, giving the horses a chance to recover some from the exertions of the attempted getaway and the dogged pursuit. Such a boring trip would usually loosen Hewey's tongue, but he'd said almost nothing all morning.

"Looks to me like that dead outlaw's weighin' on you," Baker said about midday.

"Naw," Hewey replied, "it's just that . . . Yeah, he is."

"If you hadn't killed him, he'd have killed you, and taken pleasure in the doin'."

"I've relived those few minutes over and over, and I know you're right, but somehow it won't go away," Hewey answered. "I keep seein' his expression when the bullet hit him. . . ."

"When you've relived it often enough, you'll remember the expression on his face when he thought he had you helpless. That's the one that matters. Give it some time."

"Well, while I'm doin' that," Hewey said, "along with Bradley, the other upright prisoner's name is

Clay Hawkins, and the dead one is Jesse Sloan. I got that from the shopkeeper, who doesn't eavesdrop on his customers but sure does pick up a lot of casual information. What do you reckon happened to the money they stole from the express office, by the way? They don't have it with 'em, and they sure haven't had time to spend it all."

"We could ask 'em politely, but I don't think they'd tell us," Baker opined. "On the other hand, if we play our cards right, they might show us."

"Care to explain that?" Hewey asked.

"I'm not sure just yet, but be prepared for somethin' tricky. Them two are bein' a little too meek for a couple of fellers in their position."

Hewey pondered that idea during the afternoon, conjuring up all sorts of ways it might happen but probably wouldn't. It gave him something to think about other than the dead outlaw, Jesse Sloan.

Hours before dark, Baker reined up. "Here, hold my desperado while I take a little *vuelte*," he said to Hewey, handing over the lead rope to Billy Joe Bradley's horse. He was swallowed up by trees before Hewey could ask what the hell he was up to.

Baker returned less than half an hour later, reappearing just as suddenly as he had disappeared. He took the lead rope back from Hewey and said, "Foller me."

Baker led the procession to a small, open meadow, well watered and with a good stand of grass. "We'll camp here for the night," he said.

"Why here?" Hewey asked. "Way I figure it, we could make the Henderson place before full dark."

"We're not goin' there tonight because I don't want to risk havin' you shot out of the saddle," Baker replied.

"Me? Why would I be the one shot?"

"'Cause you're the one I'm gonna send in once we get there," Baker answered. "If they're back home, Mrs. Henderson is likely to be a little touchy toward strangers showin' up, but she knows you well enough to recognize you in good light, maybe not in poor light.

"She's also not likely to be too keen on seein' these two boys again, at least not sittin' upright in the saddle. Was we to bring 'em in like that one yonder, she might be more approvin'."

Hewey could see no holes in Baker's logic, so he swung down from the saddle, keeping a firm hold on the lead rope to Hawkins's horse. Baker had already dismounted and moved to untie Bradley's shackled hands. Once Bradley was free, Baker stepped back to give him room to dismount. Bradley swung his leg over the saddle and then lunged at Baker, landing on top of the aging former lawman and grabbing the pistol from his holster.

The sudden violence startled the horses, which began a frenzied milling, blocking Hewey's view of what was happening and making it impossible for him to come to Baker's aid. The next thing he knew, Bradley had remounted, grabbed the loose lead rope, and was into the trees.

Hewey dropped his reins and his outlaw's lead rope, dodging horses to get to Baker, sprawled on the ground. He glanced up to see Hawkins spur his horse. His shackled hands were still tied, but he spurred the horse in the left shoulder to guide him toward the right. Horse and rider were quickly swallowed up by the trees, leaving Hewey, Baker, their two horses, and Jesse Sloan's loose mount. The loose horse cocked his ears forward and looked briefly as if he might follow the other two, but then turned back. Hewey could hear shouting at a distance, but the trees muffled the sound, and it soon faded away.

"Are you okay?" Hewey asked as Baker rolled over onto an elbow and tried to rise.

"Just knocked about half the air out of me, maybe twisted my bum leg a little, but I'm too ornery to hurt all that bad," Baker replied hoarsely.

Hewey helped him to his feet, but the bad leg wouldn't hold Baker's weight. "No way I can mount like this, so those boys are yours, Hewey. Go git 'em."

"I'm no gunman," Hewey protested.

"No, but you can handle a horse better'n most men," Baker said, "and you'll make good time without runnin' yours into the ground.

"Besides, you won't have to be a gunman to bring

those two back. The gun that rapscallion took off of me ain't loaded," Baker added with a big grin.

"You were figgerin' on this?" Hewey said quizzically.

"Somethin' like it."

"Well, I wish you'd told me."

"Told you what?" Baker asked. "I didn't have a hint of what they might pull, jist figgered it would happen, and I told you that much."

"Yeah, you did," Hewey conceded, "but where is it I'm supposed to make good time to?"

"Their campground. Couldn't hardly have hid that money anywhere else and hoped to find it again without landmarks. That old store was a good one. Besides, that's the only place they stopped long enough. That's what that Jesse Sloan come back for, too, not for his partners. Once he'd shot you, he probably would have shot them, and taken all the money for himself."

"I'll be damned," was all Hewey said.

"Foller the road and you should be there ahead of 'em after they take roundance, figgerin' to throw us off. Just hang back until they've dug the money up and stashed it in their saddlebags. It'll be like takin' candy from a baby. Now go on. I'll meet you back up the trail after a bit."

Hewey swung into the saddle, shaking his head and grinning. "You are a caution," he said to Baker as he reined his horse back toward the road.

Hewey struck a long trot that ate up miles without unduly tiring the horse. Now and then he would vary the pace with an easy lope, then drop back into the trot. The horse lathered up a bit at first, but Hewey thought it was more from the excitement in camp than because of exertion. Whenever he felt his mount tiring, he would ease back into a long walk, a gait the horse could maintain with apparent ease, and which fell just a little short of a trot.

The shadows were beginning to lengthen when he reached the bend in the road a few hundred yards from the old store. He had no clear sense of where his quarry might be and didn't want to chance being seen, so he pulled into the trees to the right of the faint road and passed behind the store. He circled well beyond the campsite before crossing the road and slipping back into the trees, then easing up on the camp from the far side.

The outlaws had pushed their horses hard, and despite the extra miles their looping trail had added, they were at the site within an hour after Hewey's arrival. The horses were winded, and Hewey could see from the overlapping sweat lines that they had lathered repeatedly. The nervous desperadoes began arguing over which of several dead tree trunks held the money. Eventually they settled on one, but when it turned out to be empty, the argument resumed. They got it right the second time, and Bradley stood watch with Baker's gun while Clay Hawkins retrieved the stolen money, crawling halfway into the log for the last of it. It was much more than a couple of saddlebags could hold, and came in six heavy canvas and leather satchels with padlocks. They spread the load between them and secured the bags, then remounted.

The way they strained with the bags answered a question that had nagged at Hewey ever since a search of their bedrolls and saddlebags turned up nothing. He couldn't understand why they would stash their ill-gotten gains before completing their escape, but watching them handle the bags, he realized the weight would have slowed their climb out of the canyon. The robbery netted more than Hewey had assumed, and it wasn't all paper, by any means. They evidently had intended to slip back and retrieve it when they judged that pursuit had run its course.

Retrieving it now and attempting the climb on already jaded mounts made far less sense, and Hewey figured that reason had given way to desperation after their narrow escape. It was time for him to make an appearance.

With Baker's spare Colt in his hand, Hewey threaded his way through the screening trees and out into the open.

He'd wondered what he would say at that point, and the "Hands up!" that came out of his mouth seemed a little lame for a natural-born talker, but it sufficed. Both outlaws jerked their heads in his direction, and Billy Joe Bradley quickly drew the stolen six-gun from his waistband, thumbed the hammer back, and pointed it at Hewey.

Hewey knew the gun was unloaded, and the empty chambers he could see in the cylinder confirmed it, but his throat still constricted momentarily and his heart skipped several beats. Bradley squeezed the trigger and his eyes registered surprise when the hammer fell on an empty chamber. He tried again with the same result, then a third time. By then Hawkins had his hands in the air. Bradley pitched the gun aside and reluctantly raised his own hands. Hewey ordered Bradley and Hawkins to dismount and sit, then, keeping his eyes on them, he retrieved the rope from one of the saddles by feel, shook out a loop, and deftly dropped it around the two outlaws. Jerking the slack, he tied the rope hard and fast to the saddle horn on the nearest horse.

"If either of you makes a move, I'll wave my hat at this pony's head, and he'll take both of ya for a little drag through the forest," he said, then sat on a downed tree trunk to wait for Baker. The wait was little more than an hour.

"You've captured two wanted fugitives single-handed, and without firin' a shot," said Baker as he entered the campsite from the direction of the road. Jesse Sloan's free horse trailed a little ways behind him.

"I might just make a lawman out of you yet," Baker said with a smile.

Hewey grinned, then shook his head. "This little

adventure is liable to cure any inclination I might have had in that direction," he replied. "In fact, I'm about cured already."

CHAPTER EIGHT

Baker and Hewey shepherded their charges to the nearby stream to water the horses. By their sizeable intake, Hewey judged that the outlaws' two mounts had come a long way since their last drink. Once the horses had their fill, they rode back to the campsite. All things considered, Hewey thought, those horses would have gone to the ground before they made it out of the long canyon. He had no use for anyone who would treat a horse that way.

"Might as well spend the night here as somewhere else," Hewey said, "right back where we started this mornin'. We don't seem to be makin' much headway."

"Not much," Baker agreed. "But we have the express company's money—and this time there won't be any hijinks." He directed that last part to the two prisoners. Baker remained mounted as he approached Billy Joe Bradley.

"There sure as hell won't be," Hewey agreed, releasing his coiled rope from the leather thong that secured it to his saddle and shaking out a small loop. He lofted it high enough to settle neatly over Bradley's hat and onto his shoulders. Hewey then jerked the slack and tightened the rope around Bradley's neck.

"If I get so much as a notion that you're up to somethin', I'll jerk you out of the saddle and drag you half a mile through them trees."

Hewey could hardly believe he'd just said that, and he was equally startled to realize that he meant every word of it. This amateur lawman business was getting the best of his good nature. Worse, he couldn't yet see a way to turn any of it into a funny story. By and large, there just wasn't any humor in it. After a little thought, it dawned on him that there hadn't been much to laugh about ever since he first laid eyes on Billy Joe Bradley.

Baker and Hewey set a leisurely pace the next day, once again giving the outlaws' horses a chance to recover from the previous day's exertions. That brought them to the Henderson place by late afternoon. Hewey went in alone, and soon returned.

"The Hendersons aren't back yet," he told Baker, "and I don't think they'd mind us layin' over here tonight. We could sleep pretty snug in the wagon shed, and snub these two up tight to a stout corral post."

"Gotta sleep somewhere," Baker agreed, and the small processional followed the short trail to the Henderson place.

The untying, dismounting, and unsaddling process was uneventful again, the prisoners' cooperation aided once more by Hewey's dexterity with a rope. He felt no need to repeat the previous night's warning; a rope around the neck provided a powerful reminder.

Hewey was mounted before daylight the next morning and working his way toward the back of the Henderson horse pasture. By full sunup he had the horses in the corrals and the Samuels mounts sorted off from the remaining Henderson horses. The sorting went quickly because the five Samuels horses tended to hang together out of familiarity. Likewise, the five hard-ridden Henderson mounts were quick to rejoin their herd-mates when Hewey turned them out. Up against the others, the ones he turned out looked a bit gaunt and drawn, but Hewey knew they would soon regain their bloom and go into winter in good flesh.

It was early afternoon when the small troupe reached the turnoff to the Swenson homestead.

"I reckon I best go in alone," Hewey said. "The

Hendersons ain't likely to harbor any good will toward our prisoners, and I doubt the Swensons would feel much more accommodatin'."

"Me and these boys will cool our heels here while you check on the Hendersons," Baker replied. "And while you're about it, I wisht you'd see if Mr. Swenson has a couple of shovels we could borrow until tomorrow. Your dead outlaw needs to go into the ground pretty soon, and we'll let his partners here do the honors of diggin' the hole.

"We'll go on down the trail a ways to plant him; wouldn't be right to put him around here where these good folks have to see the grave and pay him any more mind. Won't be so far, though, that you can't get back here with the shovels in the mornin' and still catch up with me and the other two in a couple or three hours."

Hewey nodded his assent and turned down the Swenson road. It wasn't far to the clearing and the Swenson house. Once he was fully visible, Hewey reined back to a deliberate walk and raised his right hand, palm forward. It was an age-old symbol of both greeting and peaceful intentions, and Hewey meant both. He could see both Henderson and Lars Swenson on the front porch. The two men rose to greet him and stepped to the front edge of the small porch, Henderson considerably more slowly than the older man.

Hewey stopped a respectful distance from the house, just as he would at a cow camp, dismounted, and led his horse forward. Seeing nothing to tie to except a porch post, he dropped his reins and hoped that the Samuels mounts had been taught the concept of standing where the reins fell. The cowboys called it "ground tied." He stepped forward to shake hands, first with Swenson and then with Henderson.

"Mr. Calloway, I presume. I'm Nate Henderson, and I owe you my life."

"No sir, Mr. Henderson," Hewey replied. "Them thanks go to Mrs. Henderson and Mrs. Swenson. All I did was drive your wagon a ways so your wife could tend to you. You're lookin' a lot better than I was afraid I'd see you at this point, so your nursin' care is even better than I expected. And the name's just Hewey."

"Call me Nate. I still owe you a big debt."

"Just heal up," Hewey said.

"I've had a lot of help doing that," Henderson replied, "and I appreciate you stopping by. It was good to meet you, and Martha will be happy to see you."

"So will Maria," Swenson added, sticking his head in the door and calling out "Maria, Mrs. Henderson! There is someone here to see you!"

The women stepped out soon, and Martha Henderson's eyes lit up. "Mr. Calloway! I am so glad to see you. Nate and I have been hoping you would stop on your way back through here."

"Yes, ma'am," Hewey said, jerking his hat off and rolling the brim in his hands. "I've been anxious to see how all of you were gettin' along. Hanley Baker sends his regards, too. He'd come himself except that we have prisoners, and we reckoned that they had no business here."

"I would as soon not see them again," Mrs. Henderson agreed.

"There's one you couldn't see if they *were* here," Hewey said before thinking. "He's wrapped up in a tarp."

"So at least one of the three won't be causing anyone further misery," said Nate Henderson. "That's good to hear."

"Which one is it?" Mrs. Henderson asked a bit apprehensively.

"Jesse Sloan, ma'am," Hewey said. "The one with the nearly black hair. Billy Joe Bradley's still alive, him and the sandy-haired one, Clay Hawkins."

"Clay Hawkins, you say? He's the one who never pulled a gun on me," Nate Henderson said. "Seemed to be trying to stop the other two, but it didn't do any good."

"Well, he goes up a notch in my estimation," Hewey said, "but just a notch. He could have ridden off and left them others any time, but he didn't. And Hanley Baker's feelin's toward him won't improve even a smidgen. He takes a dim view of outlawry, and to him the least among 'em is just as guilty as the worst he rides with. Maybe a judge and jury will take a kinder view of Clay Hawkins, but Baker never will."

"I guess it doesn't pay to offer the benefit of the doubt in his line of work," Nate Henderson said.

"No sir, I'm pretty sure it don't," Hewey replied.

The Swensons had stood back, letting Hewey and the Hendersons talk. "Mr. Calloway," Lars Swenson said at last, "Maria would like to offer you a cup of coffee. It is already brewed."

"I would gladly accept, ma'am, and thank you for the offer. Mr. Swenson, if you don't mind, I'd like to borry a shovel or two from you, jist overnight. That deceased outlaw needs to go into the ground, and them other two can dig the hole. We'll bury him down the trail a ways so as not to trouble any of you folks, and I can have the shovels back to you in the mornin'."

"Of course, Mr. Calloway," Swenson replied. "I will get them from the barn." He left at a spry trot and was soon back with two shovels.

"We're obliged to you for the use of 'em," Hewey said as he secured them behind his saddle. "And before I forget, I've got somethin' for Mrs. Henderson." Hewey untied the folded package from the rear saddle skirt, and brought it to Martha Henderson.

"It ain't much, but me and Baker thought it might brighten things up for you a bit."

Mrs. Henderson untied the sisal-twine binding and unfolded the yellowing paper. Her eyes grew wide and she raised a hand to her mouth as she saw the white sheets. "It's . . . how did . . . I don't know what to say! Thank you, Mr. Calloway! Where did you . . . Oh, my Lord!" Her eyes welled up with tears and she began to sob, smiling the whole time.

Hewey felt some sweat drip into his own eyes; at least that's what he thought it was. Maria Swenson smiled broadly and looked as if she couldn't have been any happier had the sheets been hers. Lars Swenson and Nate Henderson both smiled.

Mrs. Henderson finally regained her composure and said to Hewey, "Mr. Calloway, if Nate weren't standing here, I would give you a kiss!"

"If he wasn't standin' here I'd feel morally obliged to step backward a pace or two," Hewey said with his crooked grin.

That brought laughter from the whole crowd, including Maria Swenson, who could evidently understand a lot more English than she could speak. Feeling heat rising in his cheeks, Hewey quickly put his hat back on his head, mounted, and turned halfway toward the trail. "Sure glad to visit with you folks and to see such an improvement, but I'd best be givin' Baker a hand."

He waved, and they all waved back as he reined the horse on around, touched spurs, and loped away. Hewey hadn't felt that good in a week or two. Maybe three or four.

They caught a few hours' sleep not far down the trail, then resumed their journey as soon as it was light enough to see. After a couple of miles, Baker reined up. "This is the place. I remember it from when we first come by, on the way up."

"How could you remember that much about the

country?" Hewey asked. "We were travelin' fast and tryin' to track them three at the same time."

"It pays to know the country you're passin' through," Baker answered. "Might be important later. There's a better spot four or five miles on, but this jasper don't deserve it. I was sorta savin' that one for myself, should it come to it."

Hewey thought that sounded like a bit of a stretch, and glanced over at Baker's face. It was a little shy of straight and sober.

"If you'd wanted to be buried there, you might should have mentioned it," Hewey jibed back.

"Like you said," Baker answered, "we were pretty busy."

Baker handed Hewey the lead rope to Clay Hawkins's horse and rode slowly into the trailside clearing, circling a couple of times and looking back toward the trail. At length he stopped.

"We'll plant him right here," he announced, "far enough off the trail to be out of the way, but easy enough to be found should somebody want to claim him."

Hewey hadn't thought of that second consideration, but it made sense. The young outlaw might have family a lot more decent than he was.

They repeated the wary untying and dismounting ritual, but this time Hewey didn't bother to deploy his rope. He unfastened it and shook out a loop with a couple of coils of slack, keeping it handy and visible just in case.

With the two prisoners dismounted and Hewey's

rope still at the ready, Baker rode over to Hewey, untied the shovels, and pitched them to the ground near the prisoners. "Dig!" he ordered.

Baker and Hewey dismounted and tied the five horses to nearby trees, then settled in to wait. Hewey became restless before long and began pacing.

"Ya got ants in yer britches?" Baker asked good-naturedly.

"Just can't sit still long," Hewey said. "I gotta get up an' move."

The first of his moves was to untie the heavy canvas express bags from the horses of the two remaining outlaws and shift them to Sloan's horse; freed of its original burden, the horse could easily carry the bags, reducing the load on the other two mounts. His pacing then took him near the faint road, where he stumbled onto a broken chunk of weathered board and a small tangle of wire; he took them to be signs of an old wagon repair gone wrong. It gave him an idea for a way to pass the time while the grave got longer and deeper.

He soon scared up a couple of small deadfall limbs which he fastened into a makeshift cross with some of the wire as a binding. Lacking fencing pliers, he had to break the wire by worrying it back and forth until it weakened and snapped. He then dug out his pocket knife and whittled a point onto the long end of the cross before turning his attention to the piece of board. Carving into it was a laborious task, mainly because Hewey's limited formal education left him struggling to spell the dead outlaw's name. He took some pride in the finished product, crooked but deeply carved letters that read SLONE. With a feeling of accomplishment, he broke off another couple of pieces of wire and secured his masterpiece to the cross.

"Thisaway," Hewey said, "if his people do come lookin' for him, he won't be hard to find."

"Nope, he won't," Baker agreed, "especially if they can't read too well."

Hewey had the feeling that Baker's comment included a veiled poke at him, but he wasn't quite sure how or where.

Baker strolled over to the hole and looked in, keeping a wary distance from the two outlaws and their shovels. "It ain't near six feet," he said, "but it's deep enough for the likes of him. Drag him in there."

"I want my tarp back" were the first words Hewey had heard in a day or two from a sullen Billy Joe Bradley.

"It don't rain where you're goin'," Baker retorted. "Put him in, tarp and all."

The two living outlaws soon had the hole refilled and mounded over, it taking a lot less time to shovel loose dirt than to pry it out of the ground.

Baker tossed them Hewey's grave marker. "Hammer it in good and solid," he said, "then leave them shovels standin' in the soft dirt."

Bradley took a look at the carved inscription.

"Even I can spell better than that," he said before clamming up again.

Hewey bristled at the insult.

Once Bradley and Hawkins were mounted and tied, Hewey loosened the cinch on the spare horse. The only load it would be carrying from here on was the saddle and express bags. Baker took up the two lead ropes and angled back onto the trail, the loose horse following on its own. Hewey retied the shovels and mounted. Taking a look back at his handiwork, he struck a long trot up-trail toward the Swenson place.

It was a short ride, and Hewey once again saw both Lars Swenson and Nate Henderson on the porch as the house came into view. They waved in recognition, and he didn't check the horse's stride until he neared the porch and reined up the respectful distance away. "Mornin' to you fellas," he said without dismounting. "Mr. Swenson, if you'll tell me where they go, I'd be happy to put these shovels up for you. We sure appreciate the loan."

"Yust leave them with me," Swenson countered. "I am glad they were useful. Would you come in? Breakfast should be ready soon."

"You have no idea how much I'd love to taste some good cookin'," Hewey answered. "My cookin' and Baker's is so bad it ought to be illegal. But I need to catch up with him before one of them boys springs some trick we've never thought to look for. Billy Joe Bradley, for one, ain't got nothin' to lose. Tell the womenfolk hello for me, and I'm gonna grieve all day over my missed chance at breakfast."

Hewey handed over the shovels and turned back toward the trail, moving at a walk until he'd crossed his imaginary line of respect, then breaking into a slow lope. As he neared the tree line he turned and waved his hat in the direction of the Swenson house. He thought he could see four forms wave back.

It was late morning when Hewey caught up to Baker. The former lawman had things in hand, and Hewey decided that he had probably handled tougher situations than this one over his long career. He found himself thinking about Baker's strong sense of command, and the fact that it was readily recognized by people who had never laid eyes on him before.

Hewey had found himself in the presence of numerous lawmen over the years, some in their official capacity with him on the receiving end. They ran the gamut from bumblers who owed their jobs to politics, through thugs who had no business with authority, and finally to many competent officers of the law. But Hanley Baker stood out; Hewey put him in the same league as Sheriff Wes Wheeler back home. Their breed was rare, he was sure—mighty thin on the ground, in cowboy lingo.

Another couple of uneventful days and nights at their relaxed pace brought them within striking distance of the Samuels place. Hewey had selected the dun again when they exchanged the well-used Henderson horses for the Samuels mounts, but the Samuels horses were still recovering from their hard travel, and the dun had yet to resume his foolishness. That changed the last morning out, and the suddenness of the pitching fit almost unseated Hewey. He was forced to drop the lead rope to Billy Joe Bradley's horse, but Baker quickly took it up. Rather than stay put and watch the show, Baker led his little parade down the trail, clearly expecting Hewey to prevail and catch up.

Hewey didn't know whether to be pleased at Baker's confidence in him or put off by the former lawman's abandonment, and he was too busy at the time to think the matter through. The dun added some new stiff-legged landings to his bag of tricks, and they jarred Hewey enough to snap his teeth together. Some jumps ended on all four legs and some just on the forelegs. He also seemed to be jumping higher than he had before, but Hewey stayed astride. Eventually the dun tired and settled down. Hewey kept him at a lope for a time to take out any starch that might be left.

By the time he caught up to Baker the dun was winded and Hewey's teeth hurt.

Baker had a slight lead when they reached the turn-off to the Artie Samuels place, and that was fortunate, Hewey thought, because he would have ridden right past it. Baker's ability to memorize terrain impressed Hewey and challenged him at the same time. That skill could sure come in handy for an itinerant cowboy, and Hewey promised himself that he would make a point to brush up on his own attentiveness. He would probably begin as soon as tomorrow or the next day.

Artie Samuels was out in front of the barn when the group arrived, and Hewey could see even from a distance that he was sewing on some part of a saddle. Baker handed his lead rope to Hewey and rode in closer, giving the usual hand sign of a greeting. Samuels recognized him, stopped what he was doing, and stepped forward to shake hands. Hewey saw Baker gesture in his direction, and he saw Samuels make a sweeping gesture of welcome in return, so he led his prisoners forward.

When he arrived, Baker was well into the details of the pursuit, capture, escapes, and recaptures of the past days. Hewey missed the part about the gunfight, but he could see that its outcome pleased Samuels.

"I wish you'd had call to shoot all of 'em," Samuels told Hewey.

"I don't think my luck could have held out through that many gunfights," Hewey answered with his customary grin. "And make no mistake, it was pure luck and nothin' else that got me through the one I did have. If Baker hadn't come crashin' through those trees like a South Texas brush-popper, I wouldn't have had the chance to pull that belly gun and use it."

"Well, maybe these two will still give you cause to shoot 'em before it's all over. If not, I sure hope to see 'em hang. Mr. Baker told me what they did to the Hendersons. That's a hangin' offense in my book," Samuels said. Hewey could tell he meant it.

"What I heard from the Hendersons," Hewey answered, "was that Clay Hawkins, the sandy-haired one yonder, didn't raise his gun at them."

"Maybe the good Lord will take pity on his soul, but he was there. That makes him part of it," Samuels stated flatly. It was pretty much the same view that Baker took, Hewey recalled, and evidently no more subject to change.

Baker interrupted the conversation at that point, asking if the Slash M horses were nearby so a swap could take place in time to move on before dark.

"No need to be in such a hurry, is there?" Samuels asked. "You're welcome to spend the night right here and have a good meal in the bargain. Don't suppose you've eaten all that well on the trail."

Hewey could see Baker thinking the idea through

before answering. He hoped the answer, when it finally came, would be yes.

"We'd hate to put you to any trouble," Baker began, and Hewey considered that a prelude to accepting Artie Samuels's hospitality.

"No trouble at all," Samuels said. "I don't get much company if you discount horse thieves, so I'll enjoy havin' you two here and seein' them boys with their ears pinned back."

"Then we'll tie 'em to a corral post where you can see 'em, and sit and jaw a while," Baker said by way of acceptance. Hewey's jaw was more interested in taking on some decent cooking than in carrying on a conversation. It was a rare state of affairs, but Hewey had already taken his belt up one notch on this trip, and if he needed to do it again he'd have to carve out a new one with his pocket-knife.

"Mr. Samuels," said Baker as he and Hewey prepared to untie and dismount the prisoners, "I don't expect any trouble, but I'd feel better if your shotgun wasn't leanin' against the barn yonder."

Samuels moved quickly to pick it up. "Sorry. I never gave it a thought. After having my horses stolen, I got to where I never go anywhere without my Parker."

"That's a good practice," Baker replied. "I just have a habit of lookin' for the boogers in any situation before I wade in."

Hewey did the untying this time, and he freed Clay Hawkins first.

"Sit yer butt down by that corral post," Baker ordered Hawkins, pointing with the pistol in his hand. Hawkins did as he was told.

Turning to Billy Joe Bradley, Hewey freed his shackled hands from the saddle. He was stepping backward when Bradley gave him a vicious kick to the head. Hewey saw the boot coming in time to snap his head back. He took a glancing blow to the side of his face, but Bradley's Old Mexico–style spur left a long gash.

The world was spinning and Fourth of July fireworks were going off in Hewey's head. Anger alone drove him to grab Bradley's left arm and jerk him completely out of the saddle, slamming him to the ground on his head and left shoulder.

The next thing Hewey knew, Samuels thrust the twin barrels of his shotgun within three feet of Bradley. Both hammers were cocked, and his finger was on the trigger.

Baker stepped forward immediately, cocking his six-gun as he came, but Hewey saw that it was leveled on Samuels, not Billy Joe Bradley.

"Don't do it, Mr. Samuels," Baker warned. "I'd hate to have to shoot a good man to save the likes of Bradley, but I will if I have to. He's in my custody and under my protection until I can unload him on somebody else."

"He deserves killin'," Samuels retorted, never taking his eyes off Bradley.

"That he does," Baker agreed, "but it'll be at the direction of a judge and jury. Nobody's gonna kill him in cold blood."

"I don't see where you owe him anything," Samuels continued. "You're not wearin' a badge anymore."

"No sir, but I wore one for a long time, and the duty doesn't end when the badge comes off. I'm goin' to ask you one more time to please back away."

Samuels finally took his eyes off Bradley and turned them up toward Baker. "I believe you mean it."

"I do."

Samuels swung the twin muzzles of his shotgun upward and de-cocked the hammers, then passed the weapon to Hewey. "Keep an eye on this sorry SOB while I help Mr. Baker drag him to the post. Then we'll get that cut on your face fixed up."

Hewey thought the venison Samuels floured and fried was just about the best meal he'd ever eaten, and he wolfed down three biscuits with flour gravy. Even the coffee tasted better than what he and Baker had brewed. He knew he took special pleasure in the meal because he had been starved down, but it still tasted good even discounting the boost to his appetite.

He and Baker ate at the small kitchen table while Samuels sat out on the front porch watching the prisoners, shotgun across his lap. Hewey wasn't concerned that Samuels would repeat his actions of the afternoon; once the excitement had subsided, Samuels appeared resigned to letting the two outlaws live for a while longer. At least it hadn't interfered with the quality of his cooking, for which Hewey was especially grateful.

If Baker was concerned about Samuels, he didn't show it. He ate even more than Hewey had, and all in the same few minutes. Once they'd finished, Hewey washed the tin plates and utensils they'd used while Baker stepped out onto the porch. When Hewey joined Baker and Samuels, they were discussing feeding the prisoners.

"Me and Hewey ate like pigs at a trough, but there's still plenty left for you and them," Baker said. "You put on a pretty big bait of supper."

"I guess starving a prisoner is just about as bad as shootin' one," Samuels said in a good-natured way that surprised Hewey.

"I didn't really expect you to feel that kindly toward them two," Hewey put in.

"There's no 'kindly' in how I feel about trash such as that, but I owe you and Mr. Baker an apology for the way I acted this afternoon," Samuels answered. "I just blew plumb up thinkin' about the Hendersons, and when that Bradley kicked you in the head, it was the last straw for me. If Baker hadn't stopped me, I'd have blasted that sumbitch in two. Probably would have done the same to the other one. I'm not usually prone to that sort of thing, but sometimes it just boils up in a man."

"I'm glad it didn't come to it," Baker told him, "and you don't need to apologize. I've wanted to do the same thing several times."

"Me too," Hewey chimed in, "and I'm a natcherly friendly sort of feller. I'll sure be glad when we're shed of both of 'em. What in the world made Billy Joe Bradley kick at me and start that ruckus, do you reckon? He sure as the devil couldn't have thought he'd get away."

"I expect he was hopin' one of us would shoot him," Baker replied.

"You think he wanted to get shot?" Hewey asked. "Why in hell would he want to take a bullet?"

"He wouldn't be the first who'd rather die that way than havin' his neck jerked by a hangman's noose," Baker replied, "and he'll hang for sure after all he's done. That's a good enough reason, the way I see it, to keep him alive long enough for the hangin' to be carried out."

"If anybody deserves it, it's him," Hewey agreed, "but until then I figger I ought to go carry him and Hawkins something to eat, though I'm not feelin' real charitable about the portions."

"I'll help you," Samuels said, then paused before adding, "And leave the Parker here on the porch."

Baker brought the coffee.

While the two prisoners ate, Hewey, Baker, and Samuels relaxed in front of the barn, within easy view and earshot of Bradley and Hawkins.

"Seen a few hangin's over the years," Samuels said, loud enough to be heard twenty feet away amid scraping on tin plates. "The worst one was the time when the hangman either tied on too much weight or left a little extra slack in the drop, maybe both. Jerked that ol' boy's head plumb off. He'd had a hood on, but it come off, too, and I was close enough to see that ol' head rollin' around and the eyelids openin' and closin' for what seemed like quite a spell."

Baked nodded. "The worst ones for me, I guess, are those where the drop don't snap their necks, and they hang there kickin' and chokin' to death. Sometimes it can take a while."

The conversation continued for a while in the same vein, the stories eventually getting so gruesome that Hewey began to sense Samuels and Baker were making them up on the fly. He thought it positively shameful for the pair to be spinning such windies, positively shameful. He also hoped the stories would stop before Billy Joe Bradley caught on.

Later, when Hewey gathered up the plates, he noticed that Bradley hadn't eaten much of the venison and only half a biscuit. The waste was unacceptable, he mused to himself, but he still smiled. He hadn't realized he could be that much of a hard case.

❖

Hewey later decided that Baker had taken Samuels at his word about the afternoon excitement, because Baker didn't hesitate to accept when Samuels vol-

unteered to take a watch during the night. That
made it three short guard shifts instead of two
longer ones, and Hewey got the best night's sleep
he'd had in so long he couldn't remember. Nevertheless, he was back from Samuels's horse trap with the
Slash M mounts before good light the next morning.

The saddling, mounting, and retying routine went
off without a hitch. For days Hewey had just kept
his rope at the ready, but this time he helped en-
sure an uneventful process by dropping his loop
over Billy Joe Bradley's hat and jerking the slack to
tighten it around the young outlaw's neck. It wasn't
a hangman's noose, but it was a rope, and Hewey
intended it to remind Bradley of what awaited him.
It was also a bit of payback for Bradley's antics the
previous day; Hewey's cheek still smarted after the
spur-raking it had taken.

CHAPTER NINE

It was the second morning after leaving the Samuels place when Hewey got a sense that they were on or near Slash M country. It was nothing he could put his finger on, just a vague feeling. Hanley Baker hadn't said anything about it yet, so Hewey reasoned that either he was getting ahead of himself—or he was getting ahead of Baker. He liked the latter explanation, and grinned from ear to ear while basking in the glow of it.

"What's tickled your funny bone?" Baker asked, as the two rode in tandem.

"Huh?" was the most intelligent response Hewey could muster at the moment.

"That big ol' grin," Baker replied.

Only then did Hewey realize he'd been showing

on the outside what he was feeling on the inside. "Oh, nuthin'," he answered. "Say," he added all innocent-like, "where do you reckon we are?"

"We've been on McKenzie country ever since full daylight this mornin'," Baker answered in an off-hand way.

"Why didn't you say somethin'?" Hewey asked.

"Figgered you knew."

Hewey's grin faded as Baker pulled ahead, and for a moment Hewey thought he saw a smile on the man's face.

Hewey spent the next hour or so scanning the countryside, trying in vain to spot anything that could have helped Baker recognize the area. That's how he saw the rider upslope to the right, waving his hat in wide arcs over his head. Hewey waved back, trying not to spook the horses. The rider planted his hat back on his head and came at a lope, almost too fast for the terrain. As he came nearer, quartering to meet the small procession, Hewey could tell he looked familiar. Soon he made out the rider's face and the somewhat awkward way one leg stuck out a little.

Speedy Martin reined back as he approached, then fell in beside Hewey. "The Major will sure be glad to see you two," he said to Hewey and Baker. "He's had us all keeping an eye peeled for days now."

"We had some delays," Baker told him, "and

we've kept a slow pace once we finally got lined out."

Hewey saw Speedy eyeing Billy Joe Bradley and drawing away from him ever so slightly, doubtless remembering the outlaw's effort to kill him. "I remember this one," Speedy said, "and there was another one taking shots at me. Not the fella behind Mr. Calloway—he hung back."

"The one you're missin' is buried several days back up the trail," Baker told him. "He didn't survive his last gunfight."

Speedy's eyes widened at that, and Hewey could tell the youngster was impressed. "This is just like the Old West," Speedy said.

"Back yonder," Baker nodded at the trail, "it's *still* the Old West."

"Wait'll the rest of the boys hear this!" Speedy enthused, followed up by a low whistle. "If you fellas don't mind," he added, "I'm going on ahead. Most of the hands are in at headquarters shaping the horses up for next spring, and they'll all want to know you're coming, the Major and Mr. Rutherford, especially."

"We've got these two well in hand," Baker said. "See you along toward evenin'."

Speedy loped off, turning to look back a couple of times before he got too far away to see clearly.

❖

It was about midafternoon when Hewey spied a half dozen or more riders coming to meet them.

They rode at a long trot, and Hewey spotted Trace Rutherford in the lead. He recognized the man from the squared shoulders and the easy way he sat a horse. The others followed in a cavalry-style column of twos. Hewey was familiar with the formation because he had drilled repeatedly before the Cuban adventure with Colonel Teddy, forming such a column, fanning out into a skirmish line, and falling back into a column. He could do it in his sleep—and had a few times during grueling maneuvers; the horses knew the drill as well as the men did.

Hewey was a little surprised to see the Slash M cowboys riding in such a formation, though. He reasoned that Rutherford had found it difficult to part with his Army training even after stowing his uniform away. Or maybe it was Bryce McKenzie. Hewey suspected that it might possibly be a bit of both.

As the two groups came together, the Slash M cowboys flowed around Hewey, Baker, and their prisoners. Speedy Martin led one of the two columns, an honor of sorts, given his youth and the brevity of his employment so far. He found himself near Billy Joe Bradley, and Hewey noticed that Speedy initially held back a bit and didn't crowd Bradley the way some of the other cowboys did.

It reminded Hewey of the way many people treated a live rattlesnake. He'd seen grown men who would slap a saddle on anything with four legs and a coat of hair, but who hung back from a caged rattler. Hell, he was one of them.

It didn't take the young wrangler long to overcome his leeriness, however, and he soon pushed up closer.

Rutherford shook hands with Baker and Hewey, nodding toward the horse with the empty saddle. "Speedy tells me that fella lost a gunfight with you," Rutherford said to Baker.

"Oh, he lost a gunfight, all right," Baker replied with a wry chuckle, "but not with me. Hewey shot him fair and square while I was out thrashin' around in the brush. Guess I didn't make that clear to Speedy."

"The noise you was makin' got his attention long enough for me to pull that Colt you loaned me," Hewey said. "Otherwise, my saddle would be the empty one."

Rutherford's eyes widened a bit, and he turned to Hewey. "I can't wait to hear that tale," he said.

"I'm not sure I want to tell it to too many people," Hewey replied, "because there wasn't anything even a little bit funny about it. I can tell you and the boys, because you already know most of the story and I'd hate to leave you hangin' right at the end. Besides, if I don't tell it, Baker will. Away from here, though, it may not get much use."

Rutherford gave Hewey a long study. "We'll all be looking forward to it," he said, "and meanwhile, a couple of my boys will take over leading your prisoners back to headquarters. I'm sure you would enjoy a break from that chore. Major went to fetch the sheriff so you can turn 'em over to the law and be done with it all. He should be back to the headquarters by the time we are."

"Durango is a long ways off from headquarters," Baker replied. "I wouldn't think he'd be back until mornin'."

"He's not going nearly that far," Rutherford explained. "We have a neighbor that direction who's gotten himself a telephone. The sheriff's the one I expect to see by morning."

"That will set just fine with me," Baker replied. "I've about decided I'm gettin' too old for this lawman business."

Hewey was surprised and pleased to see Speedy Martin sidle up to Baker and take the lead rope for Billy Joe Bradley's horse. Speedy never said a word, just looked Bradley in the eye for a long spell, then turned his back, squared his shoulders, puffed his chest out a little, and raised his chin.

The Slash M is gonna need a new kid wrangler pretty soon, Hewey thought, chuckling a little, *'cause this one just promoted himself.*

The cowboy who'd sided Speedy in the column took the lead rope for Clay Hawkins's horse from Hewey, and the other hands took up flanking and trailing positions, one seeing to the loose mount with the empty saddle. Baker, Hewey, and Rutherford led the column.

"You'll want to keep a close eye on that horse,"

Baker said, turning in the saddle to address the hand with the riderless horse's lead rope. "It's carryin' the express office money, or most of it."

"I'll keep my eyes on it and my hands off," the young cowboy replied with a grin. Hewey wished he could think of the hand's name.

They made headquarters just at suppertime, which pleased Hewey immensely. "I hope you boys ain't too hungry, because I'm liable to eat enough for three," he announced to the assembled hands who'd come to gawk at the prisoners.

"Well, git in line behind me, 'cause I'm just as hungry," Baker replied. "You and me can't cook worth a damn."

"I think I'm a hair better at it," Hewey ventured.

"There's a fine line between awful and inedible," Baker countered, "and I can't swear which one of us is on which side of it."

Hewey thought that sounded about right.

"We'll tie your two prisoners to the porch posts on the bunkhouse until everybody is fed," said Rutherford, bringing the conversation back down to practical ground.

"And for the night we'll march them down to the salt house. Log walls and a solid floor, no windows, and only the front door, which is barred from the outside. They should be as secure there as in jail, but we'll keep a guard posted anyway."

"Sounds like you've thought this out," Baker replied. "I get the feelin' you've had some experience with prisoners."

"Along with Border renegades, we had the occasional bad apple in the Army," Rutherford explained, "and it usually fell to me to deal with both sorts. A man has to get a little creative and make do in the field, but this is like having a guard house on post."

Bryce McKenzie rode in as the men were eating supper, many of them scattered around on the edge of the bunkhouse porch. Trace Rutherford saw McKenzie first, set his plate down, and began walking out to meet him before McKenzie waved him off. The boss rode up near the bunkhouse, dismounted, and shook hands first with Baker, then Hewey, and finally Rutherford.

"I understand you men have brought in two of the three outlaws from the express office robbery," McKenzie said to Baker and Hewey.

"Yes sir, Major," Baker confirmed. "The third one is back up the trail a couple of days' ride. He ain't quite six feet deep, but I reckon there's enough dirt on top of him to hold his sorry carcass down."

That drew a smile from McKenzie. "I suppose it doesn't pay to engage in a gunfight with a Texas Ranger," he said.

"No sir, that's usually bad policy," Baker replied, "but in this case it didn't pay to exchange gunshots with a Texas cowboy, either." He nodded in Hewey's direction. "It was my partner brought him down, not me."

McKenzie arched his eyebrows as he turned to Hewey. "I didn't know you were a gunfighter, Mr. Calloway."

"I'm no more a gunfighter than I am a pig farmer," Hewey said with his crooked grin.

"I'm just a cowboy who got volunteered into somethin' I'm not much suited for," he added, casting Baker a mock glare.

"Ya done good, Hewey," Baker retorted with a smile. "I'd be proud to get you into another mess any time."

"You'll play hell" was Hewey's heartfelt response.

McKenzie took it all in with a look of amusement, as did Trace Rutherford and the other cowboys close enough to hear the conversation. Speedy Martin was among them, and he beamed broadly, proud to have played even a small role in such an exciting adventure.

"Major," said Trace Rutherford, "they've also recovered the express company's money."

"Most of it, anyway," Baker said. "They'd shot the lock and hasp off of one bag, but they couldn't have had the chance to spend much of it. The other bags are still locked up tight. I'd feel better about it if we had them bags in a good, secure place until we can turn 'em over to the sheriff."

"I have a safe in my office, Mr. Baker," McKenzie offered. "It is far too large for my needs most of the time, but there is the occasional exception. You're welcome to place the express bags there."

"I'd sure sleep easier," Baker told him.

Hewey and Baker helped Rutherford and a half dozen cowboys escort the prisoners to the salt house. When Rutherford swung the door open, Billy Joe Bradley immediately stepped backward.

"Git on in there!" Baker growled, giving Bradley a poke in the back with his pistol.

"There's somethin' dead in there," the young outlaw protested. "Stinks like hell!"

"It's salted hides," Rutherford said, "from the steers we kill for beef."

Baker nudged Bradley again. "You'll git used to it. Inside. Now!"

Two of the Slash M hands pitched the outlaws' bedrolls into the foul-smelling building. They closed and barred the door, leaving Bradley and Hawkins in the dark, shackled but untied for the first time in almost two weeks.

"Might need the borrow of a couple of you boys in the mornin' when we let them two out for breakfast," Baker said. "Just in case they get unruly and think they can rush us."

Baker ended up with far more offers than he needed, especially when Hewey counted himself among the crowd; he and Baker both had too much invested in the two prisoners to sit back and let others deal with them.

When they returned to the bunkhouse, Bryce McKenzie was seated in a chair on the porch. "Now I want to hear the story," he said to Baker and Hewey. Rutherford and the hands scattered themselves around the porch, all looking expectant.

Hewey deferred to Baker on the general narrative, knowing that Baker would stick to the facts, wrap things up much more quickly, and defer in turn to Hewey for the gunfight story. He spent the entire first part of Baker's narrative trying in vain to find something humorous to say. As the time for his turn approached, Hewey found himself unexpectedly nervous. That had never happened before.

"That's when Jesse Sloan made a run for it," Baker said as he led into Hewey's turn to tell the tale. "I stayed long enough to help ol' Hewey tie them other two up, then took off after Sloan, figgerin' he'd head for the high ground to climb out of the valley. When I didn't catch up to him or cut any tracks, I realized he'd doubled back on me, so I struck a high lope back toward the camp. I started hearin' gunfire just as I hit the trees, and I knew Hewey was tradin' shots with Sloan. I broke out into the open a few seconds after the last shot, and I saw Hewey standin' and Jesse Sloan crumpled up on the ground. Sure was a welcome sight.

"Now, Hewey, you tell 'em how come it turned out that way."

"I was sittin' there by the fire," Hewey began,

"when I heard hooves strikin' rocks and breakin' deadfall branches. It was just one horse, by the sound of it. I figured it was Baker, and Jesse Sloan had gotten away. Next thing I knew somebody come dartin' out of the trees and hid behind a big boulder. I grabbed my saddle gun and dropped down behind a dead tree trunk just about the time Sloan took his first shot at me. It was all mixed up after that, me shootin' at him an' him shootin' at me, neither one of us hittin' the other one. It died down several times when he reloaded and I didn't have anything to shoot at.

"I should have had the sense to reload my own gun durin' the lulls, but I'm not used to bein' shot at, and I guess I was a little too excited to think straight. Next thing I knew, I was droppin' my hammer on an empty chamber, but that didn't even register until maybe the third or fourth try. Jesse Sloan probably figgered it out before I did, because there he was, walkin' toward me, showin' his teeth, with his gun in his hand an' the hammer cocked.

"I had Baker's spare pistol tucked into my britches, but Sloan would have shot me before I got my hand on it. Right about then I figgered my time was up, an' I remember hopin' I'd done a few good things over the years to sorta balance out all the hell-raisin'. I wasn't sure I'd done enough.

"All of a sudden there was this big commotion, somebody horseback crashin' through the brush, and bein' as how I was starin' straight at Sloan, I saw him take his eyes off me and look in the direction of the noise. That gave me the chance I needed to grab the belly gun, point it in his direction, and pull the trigger. I don't even remember cockin' it, though I know I had to've done it. Baker saved me twice in that jackpot, first makin' me take the pistol, and again when he charged into camp. Hadn't been for either of those, I wouldn't be here now."

"That was a rousing good story, Mr. Calloway," said Bryce McKenzie. "I'm glad you are here to tell it."

"Not half as glad as I am, Major," Hewey answered with his crooked grin. That brought a laugh out of everyone, the first since Baker began the whole story. Up to then it had been mostly attentive stone faces, though there were some fierce looks when Baker recounted the outlaws' treatment of the Hendersons.

Bryce McKenzie was the first to speak after Baker finished the story. "In my military days we had occasion to deal with men of such low character in the field. We hanged them, usually, and if there were no suitable trees, we assembled a firing squad. Those days are behind us, however, and these prisoners will go to trial, after which I hope to enjoy watching Billy Joe Bradley dangling from a scaffold. Mr. Baker, Mr. Calloway, your outlaws will come to no harm while they are under my protection. Now good night, men, and sleep well. Trace, I trust you have posted a guard?"

"Yes sir, Major. Nothing will happen tonight."

"Very well." McKenzie strode to his house, and

Hewey retreated to the bunkhouse, where he spotted his bedroll already tossed onto an empty bed. He wasted no time rolling it out, taking off his boots, his shirt, and finally his hat. He fell asleep before he'd fully drawn his blanket up.

It was the best night's sleep Hewey had enjoyed since the Slash M crew was up on the mountain drifting horses down to lower range. He awakened twice, once when he heard Baker stirring and slipping out of the bunkhouse, and the other time when Baker returned. By the way the old lawman settled back into his bunk, Hewey gathered that there was nothing amiss at the salt house. When Hewey finally crawled out of his own bunk, the cook had coffee brewed, and he carried a steaming tin cupful out onto the porch. Nobody but the cook was stirring yet, and Hewey thought that the crew slept in late when at headquarters. It would be daylight in another couple of hours, maybe three.

Hewey blew across the scalding coffee as he strolled to the salt house by the light of a half moon. There he found the situation in the hands of one Speedy Martin.

"Mornin', Speedy. Why don't you cut your watch short an' grab a little more shut-eye?" he said. "I'm up and have nothin' else to do but drink coffee, and I can do that here as well as anywhere else."

"Mr. Calloway? I thought that looked like you comin'. Couldn't sleep?"

"I slept like a baby with a belly full of milk and all burped out. I'm just not used to lollin' around in bed this late of a mornin'," Hewey answered.

"With all due respect, sir, I volunteered to stand this watch, and I reckon I should stay and finish it."

The kid's reply gave Hewey a case of the grins, and he turned the handle of the tin cup in Speedy's direction. "In that case, here, take this coffee. It's purty well blowed, and I can start over with another'n back at the bunkhouse."

"Much obliged, Mr. Calloway. Thanks."

Hewey was developing a fondness for the spunky kid, he had to admit. It was hard to rattle the boy, and he took his job seriously. Hewey could find no resemblance between this eager youngster and the reckless young sociopath he nursemaided all the way north from Texas. He wished he'd had Speedy Martin as a helper on that trip instead of Billy Joe Bradley.

The Slash M crew had rolled out of their beds by the time Hewey returned to the bunkhouse for another cup of coffee. The cook eyed him critically when he snagged a fresh cup. "Gave the other one to Speedy," Hewey explained, prompting an understanding nod from the same wary cook.

Some of the cowboys were lining up for breakfast, and Hewey joined them. After filling a plate with bacon, eggs, biscuits, and gravy, he grabbed a fork from a wooden bin and headed straight for the salt house.

"Some of them boys looked pretty hungry, and

I was afraid there might not be anything left for you," he said as he handed the plate to Speedy.

"That was sure nice of you, Mr. Calloway," the kid said. "Around here it's usually every man for himself."

"Well, I hate to see a hand start the day without breakfast just because he stuck to business. Now I better go see that they don't eat it all before I get mine." Hewey turned on his heel and headed back to the bunkhouse kitchen.

Baker ate like a man on a mission, and he was mopping up the last remnants of his plateful when Hewey returned. He pointed his chin in the direction of the salt house. "You're kinda partial to that kid wrangler out yonder," he said.

"Yeah," Hewey answered, "he's got spunk and the makin's of a top hand."

"I reckon you was a lot like him at that age."

"Well," Hewey said with his crooked grin, "I wasn't near as polite. At his age I'd just set out to be a cowboy. Bought some factory-made OK spurs at fifty cents a pair out of a barrel and a worn-out saddle that cost the princely sum of ten dollars. My boots was run over at the heels an' leaked on the bottom, and my hat drooped down in front of my eyes from all that East Texas rain. I headed west an' drug my brother Walter along with me. Ol' Speedy yonder is ahead of where I was at this stage of the game."

Hewey's belly protested against the time he was giving to idle conversation, so he headed for the kitchen. As he came out with a full plate and more coffee, he announced to Baker, "Everybody's done and there's still enough left for them two hooligans in the salt house."

"Yeah, I reckon we ought to feed 'em again, jist to keep up the proprieties." Baker took his plate to the washtub, but as clean as he'd gotten it, Hewey doubted that it needed any more attention.

"I'll finish this in just a minute an' give you a hand!" he yelled to Baker, who was already filling plates for the prisoners, from the sound of scraping and rattling.

Hewey's finished plate hardly needed washing, either, but he slipped it into the steaming suds and took one of the two full ones off the wooden table.

"Seems like a shame to waste two biscuits each on them boys," he said, mostly to himself.

"Maybe somebody will give us a medal for it," Baker cracked back.

A half dozen Slash M hands went with them to the salt house, and Hewey could see that Trace Rutherford was already there, engaged in relaxed conversation with Speedy Martin. When the processional arrived, Hewey and Baker set the breakfast plates on a section of tree trunk that served as either a chair or a table, as the need arose. Hewey stepped to the door and Baker took up a position off to the side, where he could have a clear shot through the doorway should developments require it. Rutherford and the cowboys formed a rough semicircle around the door and back far enough to avoid blocking Baker's aim.

Hewey lifted the heavy bar and began opening the door. At the first sign of movement the door flew open, knocking Hewey to the ground. Billy Joe Bradley was doing just as Baker suspected he would, but he was doing it a lot faster than Hewey assumed it might happen. Bradley hit the ground at a run, and made for the arc of cowboys. Speedy Martin was dead center, directly in front of the door. Instead of stepping aside, Speedy bent into a crouch and drove his right shoulder into Bradley just below the breastbone. From his vantage point on the ground, Hewey could see Speedy lock his arms around Bradley's waist and hear the air gush out of the outlaw's lungs.

Bradley bowled Speedy over and landed on top of him as the two hit the ground, but the kid wrangler never relaxed his hold until Baker strode over and kicked Bradley in the ribs, rolling him onto his back. Baker drew his gun, cocked the hammer, and stuck the barrel in Bradley's left ear, but Hewey could tell from the gasping and wheezing that the prisoner would give them no further trouble for a while.

"Ya done good," Baker said to Speedy after Rutherford and another couple of cowboys pulled the kid wrangler to his feet. Speedy Martin beamed from ear to ear and began to redden in the cheeks.

Nobody helped Hewey to his feet, but then, he wasn't a hero, just a cowboy who got knocked onto his butt.

Bryce McKenzie had seen the excitement from his front porch, and stood smiling and shaking his head. Rutherford walked over to confer with him briefly, getting a nod from his boss before he returned. "Speedy," Rutherford said loudly enough for the whole crew to hear, "you're no longer the Slash M wrangler."

Speedy looked confused and a little apprehensive. Before he could say a word, Rutherford continued, "From now on you're a regular hand and drawing full wages."

"I don't know what to say," Speedy replied, "except thanks, Mr. Rutherford."

"No thanks are necessary," Rutherford said. "You've earned it."

"I'll be happy to keep doin' what I've been doin'," Speedy added quickly, "until you find somebody to replace me."

"Now it's my turn to thank you" was Rutherford's way of accepting the offer. "Shouldn't take too long once I've had a chance to get into town and spread the word around a couple or three hotel lobbies. There should be plenty of wannabe cowboys hunting a place to hole up with winter coming on."

This outfit sure runs smooth, Hewey thought, *and the bosses are decent human beings, not whatever kind of irascible critter C. C. Tarpley sprung from.*

❖

"Before you two get yer cold breakfast, I've got a little chore for you," Baker said a few minutes later to Billy Joe Bradley and Clay Hawkins. "Sit down!" He didn't give Bradley time to comply before kicking his legs out from under him. "Take off yer right boots. Now!"

As the duo tugged on their boot heels, Baker produced the third set of Bryce McKenzie's shackles. "If you don't mind, Hewey, lock these on their ankles."

That old manhunter has them two cross-hobbled to where they can't get anywhere at more than a shuffle, and with one bare foot at that, he mused. *Wonder what other tricks Baker has up his sleeve?*

Hewey judged it to be late morning when La Plata County sheriff Will Johnson arrived, trailing a packhorse and flanked by three men whose demeanor identified them to Hewey as regular deputies, not the gaggle of assorted townfolk that accompanied the sheriff the first time Hewey met him. Baker stepped away from the bunkhouse to greet them, and Hewey followed suit.

"I see the two of you are once again in the company of outlaws," Johnson said with a smile as he shook Baker's hand.

"We draw the SOBs like honey draws flies," Baker answered.

"And we'll be right proud to turn these flies over to you," Hewey added as he reached up to shake.

"There's only two live ones for you," Baker said.

"The third is a couple of days' ride back up the trail. Underestimated my partner here in a gunfight."

Sheriff Johnson and his deputies dismounted, and Baker offered coffee in the bunkhouse.

"We'll all be happy to take you up on that offer, but first I'd like to see the prisoners," Johnson said.

The two outlaws were sitting in the dirt in front of the salt house, still shackled and cross-hobbled. They were under the steady gaze of newly minted regular hand Speedy Martin. The choice of guard had been Hewey's idea.

"I imagine you recognize Billy Joe Bradley," Baker said, pointing to the somewhat banged-up prisoner, "and that other'n goes by the name of Clay Hawkins. The one we buried was Jesse Sloan."

One of Will Johnson's deputies took notes. "I've interviewed the express office manager and other witnesses to that crime," Johnson continued, "and they tell me that only two of the three took part in the robbery and shooting while the third held their horses."

"The outside man would be Hawkins there," Baker said, "assumin' the pattern holds up. They cut quite a swath as they went, stealin' horses, shootin' at anybody who challenged 'em, and nearly killin' one man, then tradin' shots with his wife while he laid outside bleedin' near to death. From what everybody's told us, Hawkins held back every time and even tried to talk the other two out of their meanness. He was there, no mistakin', but he wasn't mixed up in the worst doin's."

Baker had surprised Hewey several times, and standing up for Hawkins was another one to add to the list. *The old man is thorny as a mesquite tree and half again as gnarly . . . but he's fair.* He hoped people would say something kind like that about him when he got old, and reminded himself to work on it just as soon as he got a chance.

"All of that will go into our investigation," Sheriff Will Johnson said. "Now, where's that coffee?"

The sheriff and his deputies sat on one side of the long bunkhouse table drinking coffee and discussing the outlaws' depredations with Baker, Hewey, and Speedy Martin. Trace Rutherford sat off toward the opposite end of the long table, along with Bryce McKenzie; they had no firsthand experience to describe, so they were content to stay back out of the way and observe.

"I'm leaving the investigation of these men in the hands of my chief deputy, Frank Wiggins, here," Will Johnson announced over the rim of his coffee cup.

Wiggins acknowledged the statement and his identity by briefly raising his right hand a few inches. Hewey had already decided as much, seeing as how Wiggins was the only one at the table with a notepad and a pencil. Hewey idly wondered how far ahead of him Baker had been in identifying Wiggins as the lead investigator. Probably a lot, he thought.

Wiggins directed his first question to Speedy. "Mr. Martin, tell me what happened in your encounter with the outlaws."

"Well, sir, I had a broken leg, or I wouldn't have been around headquarters at all, but up in the high country with everybody else," Speedy began. Hewey could sense the kid's nervousness, but he also saw Speedy fighting it, meeting Deputy Wiggins's gaze firmly and struggling to keep his voice under control.

"I was putterin' around in the bunkhouse, sweepin' up, things like that. It was pretty early when I heard a commotion out in the corrals. I looked out a window and saw the three outlaws saddling fresh mounts carryin' our brand. I stepped part-ways out the door and hollered at 'em as they mounted and rode out of the gate. As they come past the bunkhouse, two of 'em held back and shot at me, but I got the door closed and barred as quick as I could."

"Can you identify who shot at you?" Wiggins asked.

"Yes, sir. I didn't know their names then, of course, but I sure got a good look at their faces. One was that Billy Joe Bradley and the other one was the missing outlaw that Mr. Baker calls Jesse Sloan."

"And what if anything did the third one do?"

"That would be Clay Hawkins. He was out a little ahead of the others and hollerin' at 'em to come on. He never fired a shot, as best I can tell. It was over in a hurry."

"Thank you, Mr. Martin," Wiggins said. "If you think of anything else, I'll be back here in a few days."

Hewey wondered exactly what that meant, but he didn't have to wait long for an answer.

"Mr. Baker, Mr. Calloway," Wiggins continued, "I want to interview the other people with firsthand knowledge of the case, and I was hoping one or both of you might go with me to help me locate them."

That caught Hewey by surprise, as did Baker's quick reply. "We'll both be happy to help," the old lawman assured Wiggins. It was the second time Baker had volunteered Hewey without bothering to ask his opinion on the matter.

"I don't know as how I can make another trip on sowbelly and venison," Hewey replied with a grimace. "I'm about starved down for biscuits."

"If it's any consolation, Mr. Calloway, I bake a decent pan of biscuits and make passable gravy," Wiggins said, letting a slight smile. "And the packhorse is carrying a full camp kit, so we won't lack for anything but firewood, which I doubt will be an issue where we're going."

"No, that's the one thing we had plenty of." Hewey grinned. "And if you can cook, well, that changes everything. I was sorely afraid Baker was about to draw another ten pounds off of me."

That got a laugh out of Bryce McKenzie at the far end of the table. "If you should lose a pound or two on this journey, Mr. Calloway, we'll pack it back on when you return. You and Mr. Baker are still riding for the Slash M, by the way, and you've been on the payroll all along. I won't tolerate horse thieves, and the two of you not only recovered our horses and those of others, but you dealt with all three thieves.

"You certainly earned your pay, and will be doing so again when you accompany Deputy Wiggins."

Sheriff Will Johnson deputized Hewey and Baker, "So that whatever you might do will be done under the color of law."

"What color were we under durin' all that chasin' and catchin' business?" Hewey wanted to know.

"If anyone should ask—and they won't—I'll say you were deputized," the sheriff answered.

Hewey mulled that over, along with the brief and matter-of-fact swearing-in ceremony. He decided there wasn't much difference between the two. As ceremonies went, being sworn in as a deputy lacked any sense of pomp and circumstance. In fact, he thought, the whole thing fell pretty flat. He'd at least expected to be given a badge.

The sheriff, his deputies, and his two prisoners departed just after a filling noon meal, having borrowed a pair of Slash M horses for their prisoners and a third for Jesse Sloan's saddle and the heavy express bags. The prisoners left sporting modern handcuffs in place of Bryce McKenzie's souvenir shackles. Hewey, for one, was glad to see them go. It lifted a heavy weight of responsibility from his shoulders, one he hadn't really felt until the shoot-out with Jesse Sloan. Until then he had been able to treat the trip like just another opportunity to see new country, albeit a bit hurriedly. Killing a man at point-blank range after giving himself up for lost changed the complexion of the situation entirely.

With Baker's encouragement Wiggins postponed their departure until early morning, after a good night's sleep and a fortifying breakfast. Hewey wasn't in on the discussion but found the outcome more to his liking than an immediate leave-taking. He would have been happy to postpone the whole thing for a week or more, but no one asked his opinion.

Nevertheless, it meant Hewey had nothing to do until supper, which felt a lot like sinful idleness. He decided he had as much right to commit such a sin as anyone else, but along toward midafternoon the inactivity began to chafe a little, so he strolled down to the corrals where he might have the opportunity to lend a hand. Mostly he sat on the top rail and watched the regular cowboys schooling young horses, but occasionally the boys ran onto a green bronc that refused to accept a rider, spilling every hand who mounted up. That was Hewey's specialty, and he had the opportunity to teach those horses that not every cowboy could be thrown every time.

Pretty much every cowboy could be thrown some time, however, and Hewey ate a large helping of dirt, all told. When the hands ran out of trouble-makers he strolled back to the bunkhouse kitchen, stopping several times to dust his clothes off with his hat. He considered himself fastidious in his appearance, after a fashion. Sweat stains, whiskers, and a rip here and there in his britches and shirt didn't count.

He was there at the bunkhouse table when Bryce McKenzie entered, looking for Rutherford. "Trace, in all the excitement I neglected to mention that you and the men are likely to see a crew of strangers in the next week or two," McKenzie said. "They will be setting some tall posts and stringing wire. Mr. Bird and I had a long visit yesterday while we waited by his telephone to hear back from the sheriff's office.

"By the time that call came through, he had convinced me of the utility of such a device, so I had him place another call, that one to the telephone office. The telephone will take some learning, but it could save a lot of travel when I need to arrange a horse sale. I suppose it is time for us to embrace the twentieth century."

Hewey wondered if the Major would have to keep a hand stationed by the telephone in case someone should take a notion to call. It would be a soft job, he thought, but not one he would want.

"I'll make sure all the boys are aware, Major," Rutherford assured him. "I knew the modern world would catch up to us eventually. At least the Army will always need good cavalry horses."

"That is my fervent hope, Trace, at least as long as we are in the business of supplying them."

Hewey was inclined to agree with Rutherford's optimistic outlook over what he took to be a more guarded assessment from Bryce McKenzie. He could see nothing on the horizon that threatened the military necessity for horses. The handful of automobiles he'd observed over the last few years—always at a safe distance—were fragile, noisy, and smelled of axle grease and oil smoke. The cavalry horse and the horse-drawn wagon had nothing to fear from those rickety contraptions, he was certain.

By midmorning the next day, Hewey resigned himself to the realization that it was going to be a quiet trip. Deputy Wiggins was not much given to idle conversation, a trait he shared with Hanley Baker. Hewey's efforts to elicit more than a few sparse words from either of them fell as flat as most of his biscuits. When noon passed without so much as a stop to brew coffee, his spirits fell as flat as his efforts at conversation. What good did it do to know that Wiggins could bake a decent pan of biscuits if he never stopped to do so?

Things took a more positive turn in late afternoon, when Wiggins pulled off the trail early. Hewey took it upon himself to drag in deadfall limbs for firewood, Baker started a pot of coffee, and Wiggins mixed up a batch of biscuit dough, allowing it time

to rise while he sliced several strips of salt pork to
fry.

Hewey liked things even better later, when he
discovered that Wiggins had undersold the quality
of his biscuits. They rivaled those of the Slash M
cook, and even approached those baked by Eve,
Hewey's sister-in-law. All in all, this trip was shaping up to be much more pleasant than the last one.

Their first stop on what Hewey had begun thinking
of as the "Interview Tour" was at the Artie Samuels
place. They found Samuels in the corrals. Through
the log rails Hewey could see about a dozen young
horses circling the middle-aged rancher as he eval-
uated the way they traveled. His double-barreled
shotgun was nearby, and he had one hand on it
by the time Hewey and Baker approached close
enough for him to recognize them. Even then he
eyed Wiggins suspiciously until the trio rode out
of the shade of the barn and the deputy's badge
caught and reflected a ray of clear mountain sunshine.

As Samuels left the corrals and strode out to meet
his company, Hewey saw that he now carried the
shotgun, but in the crook of his left arm rather
than in his right hand. It was in the nature of a
man carrying a tool rather than a man brandishing
a weapon. He shook hands first with Baker, then
with Hewey, and finally with Wiggins after Baker
introduced him.

"Let's go to the house," Samuels said. "I have most of a pot of coffee brewed, and it won't take long to heat it back up."

It also didn't take long for Wiggins to interview Samuels, who was away from the house and corrals when the three young outlaws exchanged horses.

"I ran onto the three Slash M horses on my way back," Samuels told Wiggins. "They were jaded and showed saddle marks in their sweated-down hair, so I knew they didn't just drift off their own range. I suspected what had happened, then scouted around until I found my own horses nearby. Sure enough, I was short three head. But no, I can't help you as to the thieves. Never laid eyes on 'em."

"That's what I'd heard," Wiggins said, "but I had to hear it from you before it was official. I'll also need a sworn statement for the court. Enforcing the law these days is some different than it was in the past."

"That's what I gather," Samuels replied, "but I still live in the past up here. Anyway, I hope I can treat you boys to some fresh venison and put you up under a roof tonight. This time of year it can chill a man clear through when the sun goes down, and that happens early in these mountains."

Hewey quickly accepted on their behalf before Baker or Wiggins—probably both—could decline the offer. As they were leaving at daylight, Samuels shook hands again all around. He spoke directly to Baker. "I'd sure like to know how the Hendersons are doing. They're good people, the sort of young blood we need in this country."

Baker nodded toward Hewey. "Ol' Hewey here made a special project of them folks. He'll be able to tell you all about 'em when we come back by here."

"I'll make a point to fill you in," Hewey said.

It was late of an afternoon when they neared the grave of Jesse Sloan. Hewey was proud of himself for recognizing the site before Baker announced it— barely. Wiggins detoured off the trail to examine the grave, but Hewey could see it well enough at a distance, and so could Baker, apparently.

"Have I been spelling his name wrong all this time?" Wiggins asked when he returned.

"No," Baker replied with a chuckle, "that was Hewey's whittlin' job, and his education was a little spotty."

"I wisht you'd told me at the time," Hewey said indignantly.

"You never asked," Baker answered. He was right, Hewey had to concede, but the whole affair left him a little ill humored, mostly at himself. He felt better after another good supper.

Baker reined up as they approached the Swensons' clearing. "Let's let Hewey go in ahead of us," he recommended. "The Swensons know him best, and he can wave us in once they've recognized him and howdied."

Wiggins agreed, so Hewey took the lead and went on at a long trot while Baker and Wiggins came at a walk. As he entered the clearing, he could see Lars Swenson sawing firewood. The woodpile, Hewey noted approvingly, was near the house, meaning Swenson wouldn't have far to carry the pieces he'd cut and split. That fit nicely with Hewey's notion of conserving energy when performing any task that couldn't be done from the saddle. He raised his right hand in greeting, and it didn't take long for Swenson to recognize him and return the gesture.

"Maria!" Swenson called out to the house, "Mr. Calloway is back!"

Hewey rode up, leaned down to shake hands, then motioned back over his shoulder. "Hanley Baker is out yonder, along with a deputy. The deputy wants to talk about the Hendersons."

"Too soon they left, Maria says, but they would stay no longer. Martha—Mrs. Henderson—she drove the wagon, but Mr. Henderson sat up beside her, not in the wagon bed. Maria still worries over him. Please, call in Mr. Baker and the deputy. We will be happy to tell you what we know."

Lars Swenson was well along in years and a bit stooped, but Hewey thought he would be imposing were it not for his good humor. He also impressed the Texas cowboy by speaking two languages in addition to the one he grew up with. Hewey could understand some Spanish, given its prevalence in his own stomping grounds, and he could make himself understood as well, after a fashion, but he was limited to words and phrases having to do with cow work—and food. Lars Swenson, on the other hand, could translate his wife's Spanish into English, neither language his own, and he could do so on almost any subject. For her part, Maria Swenson clearly understood some English, but seldom trusted herself to answer in that tongue, and often waited for her husband to translate questions that she wasn't certain she understood clearly.

It was an awkward way to conduct an interview, but Deputy Frank Wiggins was undeterred. He and the Swensons talked for a long time in that manner as Wiggins fleshed out his report on the Hendersons and their ordeal. Most of the questions involved Nate Henderson's wounds and Maria's treatment of them. Hewey and Baker stayed out of it, having given their accounts to Wiggins days before and having little or no personal knowledge of what went on between the Hendersons and the Swensons.

"We'd best send Hewey on ahead again," Baker told Wiggins as they approached the Henderson turnoff. Wiggins acknowledged the recommendation with a nod of his head.

Hewey touched spurs lightly to his Slash M mount

and moved ahead at a long trot. He found Nate Henderson slowly and laboriously sawing firewood as he entered the broad clearing and slowed to a walk, waiting for Henderson to catch sight of him. It didn't take long; Henderson was observant. He moved toward a saddle gun leaning against the woodpile, then stopped as he recognized Hewey and waved a broad welcome.

Henderson called out to the house just as Lars Swenson had, and in a minute Martha Henderson stepped through the front door, drying her hands on her apron. She smiled widely and stepped down from the porch as Hewey reined up near her husband.

"What a wonderful pleasure to see you, Mr. Calloway! I didn't know if we'd ever get the chance again."

Hewey swung down from the saddle, tipped his hat to Martha Henderson, and shook hands with Nate Henderson. "I'm here with Baker and a deputy. The deputy is investigatin' the crime spree of those three young outlaws, and he wants to interview the both of you for his report," Hewey said.

"We'll be glad to help," Nate Henderson replied.

Baker and Deputy Wiggins entered the clearing about then, and Hewey and the Hendersons all three waved them in.

Hewey and Baker for the first time heard Nate Henderson's own recounting of being shot and left for dead. "I remember thinking," Henderson told Wiggins, "that as hot as that lead was, at least maybe it cauterized the wounds. Now that's a strange thing to go through a man's head, lying there on the porch bleeding to death."

Martha Henderson's recounting of standing off the outlaws with her husband's saddle gun was brief and matter-of-fact, it seemed to Hewey, almost as if she did that sort of thing every day. The only nod to her excited mental state came when she described her plans to hitch a team that was still out in the pasture.

"I was frantic with worry," she told Wiggins, "and really wasn't thinking straight. If it hadn't been for Mr. Baker and Mr. Calloway, Nate would have died there on the porch. I could never have found the horses afoot, much less driven them to the pens, and I could never have lifted Nate into the wagon alone, even if I'd done all the rest."

The five of them stepped out onto the porch after Wiggins concluded his interviews, and only then did Hewey truly notice the bloodstains on the floorboards. It was a lot of blood, and Hewey glanced at Nate Henderson as if to reassure himself that the man was truly standing among the living. The Bible talked of miracles and Hewey had assumed those were things of olden times, that he would never see one himself. Now he wasn't so sure.

As the trio prepared to leave, Hewey nodded toward the firewood stacked on the Hendersons' porch. "I don't know how much firewood it takes to make the winter up here, but it sure looks like you're a bit shy. These boys can probably spare me for the last leg of the trip, and I'd be happy to stay and help you saw logs. You shouldn't be doin' all that much in your condition, anyway."

"Follow me," Nate Henderson smiled, crooking his finger and walking toward the back of the house. Hewey hurried to catch up, and as they rounded the corner he rocked back on his heels. There stood several cords of wood—sawn, split, and stacked.

"I'll be damned," he exclaimed. "How . . . ?"

"I spend a good part of the year cutting firewood," Henderson told him. "What's on the porch is just for these cool nights. Once it really gets cold, I'll be drawing from these ricks. What you see on the side of the house is all I have left to finish."

"Still," Hewey said, "it don't seem like you should be doin' so much in your condition. Mrs. Swenson would really give you a talkin'-to." He looked around to see that Martha Henderson wasn't within earshot, then added, "That woman might even haul off and kick you in the butt."

Nate Henderson laughed. "I expect she would, at that. Mr. Calloway, all that time I was laid up, I was wasting away. Got so weak I could hardly stand up and walk. Since we've been home I'm gradually coming back, and this pile of firewood is just what I needed to turn things around. I started out slow and went on from there. I feel a lot more like myself."

"You Hendersons are both tough, that's all I can say," Hewey replied as they walked back around.

Hewey retightened his cinch, stepped up into his stirrup, and swung into the saddle. Wiggins and Baker had already mounted.

The remainder of the "Interview Tour" was uneventful. Wiggins questioned the owner of the ramshackle store just to clarify the identities of the three outlaws, and he got the same names Hewey and Baker had heard. At the outlaws' former camp, Baker and Hewey walked Wiggins through the initial surprise capture of Clay Hawkins and Billy Joe Bradley as well as the escape and later return of Jesse Sloan. Hewey pointed out the chips and lead smears his carbine had left in Sloan's boulder and the gouges Sloan's bullets had made in the log Hewey lay behind. Wiggins asked where Sloan was standing when Hewey shot him and Hewey led him to the location. When Wiggins brushed away a layer of pine needles, he saw the black, crusted puddle of Sloan's blood.

"You were right on the mark," Wiggins said.

"A man tends to remember the worst wrecks he gets himself into," Hewey answered, "and that was shapin' up to be my worst and my last until Baker came crashin' through the trees."

"I've been in a few memorable jackpots myself," Wiggins agreed.

Finally, Baker showed the deputy the hollow log

where Hewey found the two surviving outlaws retrieving the express bags. Just for good measure, Hewey got down on his hands and knees and peered inside to be sure they hadn't overlooked one.

They hadn't.

CHAPTER TEN

The Slash M headquarters was bustling when Hewey, Baker, and Deputy Wiggins rode in. The days were definitely getting shorter, and there was still horse and cow work to be completed before winter. Hewey looked forward to staying in one place for a change after all those trail miles, and that in itself surprised him a little when he thought about it.

The biggest news was the new telephone on the wall in Bryce McKenzie's office. The Major had placed a few calls initially to familiarize himself with the gadget, Trace Rutherford said, but mostly it just hung there on the wall, a newfangled novelty with less utility than initially assumed.

Until it rang.

Hewey had been back a week, maybe ten days;

as usual, he wasn't keeping track. McKenzie's office windows were open to the cool mountain air, and the telephone bell was loud enough to be heard across the headquarters compound. Even Hewey heard it, and he was fully engaged staying aboard a green and rebellious bronc at the time.

When Bryce McKenzie emerged from his office a few minutes later, he crossed to the bunkhouse and rang the cook's dinner bell. The hands put aside what they'd been doing and gathered on the bunkhouse porch.

"A date has been set for the trial of our young horse thieves," McKenzie said. "It will commence October twentieth. I'm declaring a holiday for as long as it lasts, and we will be taking the chuckwagon with us."

Whoops went up among the cowboys at the idea of a paid trip to Durango, even if only for a day or two. Hewey thought it would be best if the stay were brief, because every day gone would mean a day's delay in starting the fall works, which might mean finishing up in the snow.

I must be gettin' old, he thought, *to come up with such a notion*. He decided to blame it on all the responsibility he had shouldered ever since he rode away from Alvin Lawdermilk's place in the spring, and promised himself that he would avoid such foolishness in the future.

"Mr. Baker, Mr. Calloway, and Speedy, the sheriff asked that the three of you be available to testify," McKenzie continued, "and I took the liberty of agreeing on your behalf. I hope you don't mind."

All three pronounced their willingness, though Hewey privately wished other people would quit volunteering him for things, even if they were things he wanted to do.

"The sheriff also said he would be sending a deputy to notify those up the trail who had an interest in the matter, but I told him we would send someone from here and cut a day off the journey in both directions."

Hanley Baker quickly volunteered to make the trip. "All these other boys are more help to you than a stove-up old feller like me," Baker reasoned. "Besides, those folks all know me now, and I won't be some stranger ridin' up. A young feller he don't know stands a good chance of catchin' a load of buckshot from Artie Samuels these days."

"Understandably so," McKenzie replied. "I'll leave it to you as to when you wish to start."

"First thing after breakfast in the mornin'," Baker said. "That'll be the last good meal I get for a few days."

"I'm sure glad you didn't volunteer me to go with you this time," Hewey said in all sincerity, which brought sympathetic laughter from most of the hands.

"Why, Hewey," Baker said with mock surprise, "I thought you were always wantin' to see new country."

"That particular country has lost its 'new' after two trips up and back," Hewey retorted, prompting more laughter from the cowboys. "I'd jist as soon stay put and top off green horses for awhile."

Hewey was startled to see Baker ride up to the corrals after an absence of only two days. "What happened to you?" he said by way of greeting. "Did ya git homesick or hungry, or both?"

"None of the above," Baker shot back with a grin. "Artie Samuels fed me good, put me up for the night, and then sent me back. He said he'd carry the message from there. He'd been itchin' to go check on the Hendersons anyway, but he didn't want to intrude. Carryin' the message would give him just the excuse he was lookin' for. Can't say I tried to talk him out of it, because the farther I went, the more I decided you were right; that trail was feelin' a little stale."

Bryce McKenzie moved payday up to the day before the crew was scheduled to leave for the trial. Each cowboy, as usual, received his cash in an envelope, and as usual, they received McKenzie's encouragement to leave most of their pay in the envelope and take only part of it with them to spend in town.

"Cowboys, like soldiers, are typically young men," McKenzie explained to Hewey and Baker, "and like young men anywhere, most have little judgment when it comes to money. I encouraged my troopers to set some pay aside before they frittered it all away in town, and I do the same with these boys. Most of them have learned the hard way that it's a good idea."

His hands usually kept what savings they had with their belongings in the bunkhouse. There was no thievery. "They know I won't tolerate it," McKenzie said firmly. This time, however, with everyone gone, the Major recommended leaving their money in his office safe. Most of them took him up on it.

"I'll leave all of mine," Hewey told him. "I ain't had a chance to spend what I already had, and that's more than enough to buy me such a good time that I regret it for weeks."

Hewey had cowboyed for a big ranch in the Davis Mountains of West Texas one year, and just before the Fourth of July the whole outfit—chuckwagon and all—decamped for the Pecos rodeo. Everybody wore the best clothes they had and even shined their boots. It was quite a parade. The Slash M entourage heading for the trial in Durango reminded him of that except for the jackets and coats they wore, clothing that would have been sorely out of place in West Texas on Independence Day.

The Slash M boys had even bathed in a galvanized tub in the bunkhouse kitchen, all of them,

including Hewey, though he held out until the end;
he was pretty sure he'd bathed no more than two,
maybe three weeks before. Baker insisted it had
been at least a month, finally shaming Hewey into
the tub. By then so many cowboys had bathed that
Hewey felt as if he were scrubbing up in a mud puddle. He was pretty sure he came out dirtier than
when he'd gone in.

Bryce McKenzie had used his new telephone to
call ahead to the wagonyard and reserve space in
an open area behind the corrals, so when the crew
arrived they had nothing to do but pull in and set
up camp the same as they would have on the Slash
M range. It was late afternoon when the crew remounted and headed for the nearest drinking establishment, all laughing about the big night they
were going to have and a few acknowledging that
the next morning would almost certainly be less en-
joyable.

Rutherford was the last to mount, and he circled
by Hewey and Baker as they positioned their bedrolls. "I need to go along with them to mother-hen
the brood and see that no one embarrasses the
Slash M. Some of those boys are too young to have
learned their limits," he said. "I'd be glad to stand
the two of you to a drink."

"I'll be glad to accept the offer," Baker replied,
"but I figger we might should drop by the sheriff's
office and let him know we're here."

"No need," Rutherford said. "The Major borrowed the wagonyard's telephone and called him. Now that he has one himself, he sure seems taken with such a modern convenience. Now, how about those drinks?"

"I'm about half ashamed of myself for thinkin' this," Hewey answered, "but I probably oughta stick to beer so I can be clearheaded enough tomorrow if I'm called on to testify."

"Oh, you can count on bein' called up to that witness box," Baker assured him.

"Lord, but responsibility sure sits heavy on a man," Hewey observed with a rueful shake of his head. "Don't think I ever realized that until this trip. It ain't been the vacation I was countin' on."

Rutherford and Baker laughed at Hewey's expression of discomfort. Both of them had learned the lesson years before, one with a badge on his chest and the other with three stripes on his sleeve.

"You've sure been a late bloomer," Baker said to Hewey.

"If it was up to me," Hewey answered in all seriousness, "I'd just as soon not bloom a'tall."

Hewey and Baker found Trace Rutherford sitting alone at a table near the wall, nursing a beer and keeping an eye on the younger Slash M cowboys. He wasn't frowning yet, which Hewey took as a sign that none of his charges had gotten unruly so far.

"The boys look to be mindin' their manners," Baker said to Rutherford as he pulled back a chair and sat down.

"That's because they know my rule: if I have to drag any one of them out of here, they're all coming. It's a little harsh, I admit, but it's the same rule I had for my troopers, and it worked. The Major's command was never embarrassed, and it's saved the Slash M's reputation as well."

"Have any of 'em ever bowed up on you?" Hewey asked.

"Only one, a few years ago. I fired him on the spot," Rutherford answered while motioning for the bartender. "He ended up at a table alone, where he counted his change and then nursed one beer for the next two hours, shaking his head the whole time. The other boys avoided him like he had a case of scabies. I hired him back after he'd sobered up, and we haven't had a problem since."

Hewey grinned and shook his own head. "With tactics like that it's a wonder the Army didn't make a general outta you, colonel at least. I'll have that beer now, and raise a toast to you."

"I'll do the same," Baker said with a chuckle.

"I'll join you two in that toast if you'll make it to the Major instead for giving me wide latitude in solving problems."

"To the Major!" they all said when the beers came, and they were almost in unison. Hewey was enthusiastic but half a beat behind the others.

Hewey sensed a much different mood in the courtroom at this trial compared to the one he'd wit-
nessed and participated in months earlier. This case
included a cold-blooded murder and two attempted
murders, along with grand theft and a spate of horse
thievery.

All in all, the crowd struck him as somber bor-
dering on grim. He hoped Billy Joe Bradley was
seeing what he himself saw, and from Bradley's demeanor he thought such was the case. The kid sat
with slumped shoulders and none of the bravado he
had exhibited weeks and months earlier.

The change had begun after Hewey's brief gunfight with Jesse Sloan and intensified after Bradley's
escape and recapture, but the sense of helplessness
and fear of what awaited him was pronounced as
the young outlaw had entered the courtroom in
chains. Hewey took pleasure in it, maybe more than
he himself considered proper. Well, if it pleased him
too much, he thought, so be it. Billy Joe Bradley deserved all he had coming to him.

Clay Hawkins was quiet and subdued as well,
but Hewey sensed no desperation in him. Hawkins
was part of the criminal trio but had no hand in the
murder or attempted murders committed by Bradley and Sloan. It was a fair bet that no hangman's
noose awaited him, just a long stretch as a guest of
the state.

The prosecutor's opening statement was brief and to the point.

"We will show that the two defendants engaged in a crime spree that included three instances of multiple horse theft in addition to the much more serious charges of cold-blooded murder, grand larceny, and at least two attempted murders."

Billy Joe Bradley's defense attorney, J. Pinkney Dobbs, declined an opening statement.

"Why do you reckon he did that?" Hewey whispered to Baker.

"I don't figger he could think of any lie big enough to make a difference," Baker whispered back.

"Somethin's been wartin' me ever since the first trial," Hewey whispered again. "Who is payin' that lawyer? And who sent Bradley's bail back then?"

"I may still make a lawman outta you," Baker said with a grin, "'cause you're thinkin' like one. And like me, it bothers you not to have an answer."

Clay Hawkins had a defense attorney of his own, and his attorney laid out a simple opening statement. "My client acknowledges his part in the horse thefts and larceny involving the stolen express money. For those crimes he throws himself on the mercy of the court. We will show, however, that he had no hand in any other crimes committed by Billy Joe Bradley and the late Jesse Sloan."

"Who's payin' *this* lawyer?" Hewey whispered.

"Talkin' around, I found out that Clay Hawkins has family in this area," Baker answered, "so I don't think his lawyer is as big a question mark as J. Pinkney Dobbs representin' Bradley."

"You don't suppose Bradley has family hereabouts, too?" Hewey asked.

"From what I've heard," Baker replied, "he's never had family anywhere, just slithered out from under a rock one day and started rattlin' his tail and strikin' at people."

Hewey pondered that for a moment, then said mostly to himself, "That doesn't answer any questions, but it sounds about right."

The prosecutor began with the meat of his case, calling his first witness.

"Would you tell the court who you are?" the prosecutor asked.

"My name is Ben Phillips, and I manage the express office at Trammell Junction" was the reply.

"And would you describe what happened on the morning in question?"

"I was in my private office when I heard a commotion in the front of the building," Phillips began. "Two masked men were demanding that my clerk, Walt Jenkins, open the safe. Mr. Jenkins did not know the combination, and told them so, at which point the two intruders opened fire, killing Mr. Jenkins immediately. They then trained their guns on me. Not wanting to meet the same fate as Mr. Jenkins, I reluctantly opened the safe. There were numerous items in the safe, but they took only the eight express bags, filled mostly with payroll money for several mines."

Hewey turned quickly to Baker. "Eight? We only found six. Do you reckon we could have missed two?"

"No," Baker whispered. "Remember that Billy Joe Bradley and Clay Hawkins dug those bags out themselves. They sure as hell wouldn't have left any behind. Besides, we went over that campsite with Deputy Wiggins. There was only six."

"So what happened to the other two?"

Baker just stared at Hewey, waiting for the idea to form on its own.

"They left them with somebody," Hewey said after a long pause. It was part question and part statement. Hewey's eyebrows went up. "That would explain a lot."

The prosecutor was still questioning Phillips. "Can you identify any of the men involved in the shooting and robbery?"

"One of them is sitting over there," Phillips replied, "the one referred to as Billy Joe Bradley. The other one, I understand, is dead now."

J. Pinkney Dobbs then got a chance to question Phillips. "You said the two men in question were masked, as I recall. How, then, can you testify that my client was one of them?"

Hewey didn't like the smug look on the attorney's face, but he recalled that same expression early in the first trial and the look of helpless failure when his case fell apart later.

"Because they lowered their masks outside, after they had secured the express bags and were remounting their horses. I got a good look at them then, along with the accomplice who had remained outside, holding the horses."

Dobbs had no further questions, and the attorney for Clay Hawkins arose. "Mr. Phillips, that accomplice was my client, was he not?" he concluded with a sweeping gesture toward Hawkins.

"Yes, he was."

"And at any time did my client enter the express office?"

"No, I didn't even know there was a third man until I slipped to the front window and watched them all mount and ride away."

"Thank you, Mr. Phillips," the attorney said. "I have no further questions."

The prosecutor presented several additional witnesses who identified Billy Joe Bradley and Clay Hawkins as two of the three men who fled from the street in front of the express office following several gunshots.

Dobbs cross-examined one of the first of those witnesses, a burly blacksmith named Carson. "Are you absolutely certain my client was among the three riders you saw?"

"I am."

"Could it be your eyes deceived you?"

"Not a chance. My hearin' may have faded a bit after all these years of hammerin' iron, but my eyes ain't lost a step. It was him, all right."

The attorney paused briefly, then took a different tack. "I recall you saying that the men you saw rode south, toward New Mexico. These men were taken hostage at gunpoint many days' ride north of here. How do you explain that?"

"Do you know how to turn a horse around?" Carson asked with one eye nearly closed and the other boring straight in on the attorney.

"Of course."

"Well, I reckon them boys do, too."

The prosecutor's questioning of witnesses took up most of the rest of the morning with Billy Joe Bradley's attorney trying in vain to undercut any of them.

The judge recessed for two hours as noon approached.

Hewey and Baker headed for the Slash M wagon to eat and ran into Bryce McKenzie and Sheriff Will Johnson along the way. "What was all that about eight express bags?" Baker asked Johnson. "We only found the six we turned over to you."

"I have a theory about the remaining bags," Johnson replied, "but I have no way of proving it. Yet."

"Me and Hewey have a theory, too," Baker said.

"We do?" Hewey asked, but no one paid any attention.

"I have a strong feeling that your theory and mine would sound a lot alike," the sheriff said, leaving the matter hanging, or so it seemed to Hewey.

Then it was Hanley Baker's turn in the witness box. The prosecutor elicited testimony about Baker's long years in law enforcement.

"Why did you volunteer to take up pursuit of the horse thieves, Mr. Baker?" the prosecutor asked.

"Because by the time Major McKenzie could have sent someone for the sheriff and brought him back, the outlaws would have had too long a lead to catch them. Mr. Calloway and I, on the other hand, were ready to start as soon as we'd swapped for fresh horses."

"Did you intend to capture the thieves, Mr. Baker?" the prosecutor asked.

"Not at first," Baker answered. "Our first priority was to get the Slash M horses back, and the rest of it just come out of that. I long ago found that what starts out as one sort of case can change a lot. It can all hang on a simple detail."

"And what if any detail changed this pursuit?"

"It was the man they stole another remount from, Mr. R. T. Samuels," Baker explained. "They rode them Slash M horses nearly into the ground before they found another three head to steal. When we trailed 'em to Mr. Samuels's place, he told us about a young couple further up the trail, Mr. and Mrs. Henderson. He was sorely worried about what them three might do to 'em. That's when it stopped bein' just about three stolen horses. Mr. Calloway and I had to go on then, and hope we could stop somethin' worse than horse thievery from happenin' to the Hendersons."

"And were you able to do so, Mr. Baker?"

"No," Baker said, "we were too late. When we rode up to the Henderson place, we found Mr. Henderson shot up awful bad, and Mrs. Henderson needed help to save his life."

"And what did you do then?" the prosecutor asked.

"Hewey . . . Mr. Calloway took the Hendersons to a healin' woman back down the trail a ways," Baker said, "while I went on after the outlaws. By the time I caught up with 'em, they'd made themselves a camp and were restin' the horses for a couple of days before climbin' up and out of the canyon."

Billy Joe Bradley's lawyer rose to question Baker then.

"Mr. Baker, you said the horses you were following had 'been run almost into the ground' by the time you reached the Samuels ranch. As you were not there until later, how can you say what state the horses were in at any given time?"

"Manure," Baker said.

"Manure, Mr. Baker? Please explain that remark."

"Manure," Baker repeated. "There wasn't none. When a horse quits leavin' manure, it's because he hasn't had anything to make manure out of. Them boys come right close to findin' themselves afoot. Besides, when we found the horses, they showed how bad off they'd gotten."

"Did you see my client with your own eyes?"

"Not until later, when I caught up with 'em."

"So you can't say with certainty that my client was among the men you had been following?"

"I can't say for certain that Billy Joe Bradley ain't Lucifer himself," Baker responded with a glare, "but I can say they're kin."

That remark brought murmurs of laughter from the crowd, and Dobbs knew he'd been whipped. He sat down and passed Baker off to Clay Hawkins's attorney, who had no questions.

The remaining witnesses offered mostly indirect testimony.

R. T. Samuels established a second horse theft charge following the three head stolen from the Slash M. Dobbs challenged Samuels's account.

"As I understand it, Mr. Samuels, you were else-where and thus cannot say for certain that my client was present when your horses were taken. Is that correct?"

"Only partly," Samuels answered. "I can say for certain that somebody left behind the stolen Slash M horse that your client was ridin' when he left there. And I can say that my horses turned up at the Henderson place, where your client committed heinous crimes before stealin' the Henderson horse he was ridin' when he was caught. Is that good enough for ya?"

J. Pinkney Dobbs had no further questions.

Lars and Maria Swenson were the next witnesses, Lars Swenson serving mostly as an interpreter for his wife. The prosecutor used her testimony to establish the nature and number of Nate Henderson's gunshot wounds and his physical condition. Maria Swenson's testimony came through clenched teeth, and Hewey thought he could feel the heat of her anger where he sat almost twenty feet away. She spat out one final word at Billy Joe Bradley as she rose from the witness chair:

"*Perro!*"

Hewey's Spanish was spotty, but he knew that meant *dog*.

Then it was Hewey's turn.

"Mr. Calloway," the prosecutor began, "you've heard Mr. Baker describe your pursuit of the three outlaws—"

"Objection!" yelled J. Pinkney Dobbs. "It has not been established that my client, Mr. Bradley, was involved in outlawry."

"Stealing other people's horses qualifies in my book," the judge replied. "Objection overruled."

"Mr. Calloway, let us save the court's time and stipulate that you delivered the Hendersons to the Swenson place. Would you describe Mr. Henderson's condition when you arrived there?"

"Mr. Henderson had lost a lot of blood and was feverin' bad when we got there, but Mrs. Swenson was able to break the fever with her herbs. She can sure work miracles. By the time me and Baker made it back there maybe a week later, Mr. Henderson was sittin' up in the sunshine and even movin' around a little. That night I'd thought he was a goner for sure."

"Could you tell the court what happened after you left the Swensons and caught up with Mr. Baker?"

"We snuck up on the camp of them three hooligans and took 'em by surprise, but while we were puttin' shackles on 'em, Jesse Sloan broke and run. Next thing we knew, he was mounted and gone. Baker stayed long enough to help me get the other two snugged up to a tree, then he went after Sloan."

"And what happened then, Mr. Calloway?"

Hewey described Sloan's return and the shootout, taking care to keep his story accurate, an unaccustomed struggle.

"Thank you, Mr. Calloway," said the prosecutor. "And did you have the stolen express bags at that time?"

"No, sir. That came later, after we'd been back a ways on the trail." He described Bradley and Hawkins's brief escape and recapture, along with the recovery of the six express bags.

"Thank you again, Mr. Calloway," said the prosecutor. "Your Honor, I have no further questions of this witness at this time."

Dobbs stood up then, puffed out his chest, and said to Hewey, "You and Mr. Baker both spoke in terms of capturing my client. Don't you mean you kidnapped him? He was a private citizen going about his lawful business when the two of you accosted him at gunpo—"

The judge slammed down his gavel and interrupted.

"Your client was a fugitive from justice," he growled. "He failed to appear in this very court, where he was sentenced to serve ten years in prison!"

"I have no further questions, Your Honor," the chastened lawyer said quietly.

The attorney for Clay Hawkins arose and addressed Hewey. "Mr. Calloway, both you and Mr. Baker have testified as to a vicious attack on Mr. and Mrs. Henderson. Would you tell the court how the Hendersons characterized my client's actions during that attack?"

"I object!" yelled Dobbs. "Only the alleged victims of this alleged attack should be asked that question, and I've heard nothing of their presence."

He'd no sooner uttered those words than the tall doors at the rear of the courtroom parted, and the Hendersons entered, accompanied by Chief Deputy Frank Wiggins.

"Ask and ye shall receive," the judge said to J. Pinkney Dobbs with a smile. "I believe your 'alleged' victims have arrived."

"Your Honor, could we have a brief recess to consider this development?" asked the prosecutor.

"I'll do better than that," the judge replied. "As the afternoon is well along, this court is dismissed until eight a.m. tomorrow."

No one thought to dismiss Hewey, so he sat dutifully in the witness chair even as the courtroom was emptying. Baker finally motioned for him to step down. Hewey looked around for official permission from the judge, and found that even he had left.

Nate Henderson was the prosecutor's lead witness the next morning. He described his brief shoot-out with Bradley and Sloan, clearly identifying both of them. Before Billy Joe Bradley's attorney could do so, the prosecutor asked him for the record if there might be any chance that his identification was mistaken.

"No, sir, not the slightest. When you are certain that you are going to die, your last memories are crystal clear," Nate Henderson testified.

J. Pinkney Dobbs waived cross-examination.

Clay Hawkins's attorney asked the same question he asked of others: "Mr. Henderson, did my client participate in the attack on you?"

"No," Henderson said, "he did not. He was encouraging the other two to stop. Actually, it was more like begging."

Martha Henderson's testimony buttressed that of her husband. She marveled that she hadn't been shot herself, and speculated that she'd simply made a smaller target, kneeling by her husband's body. The prosecutor challenged her identification, as he had her husband's.

"I will see the faces of those two young men as clearly on my last day as I saw them then," she stated. Throughout her brief testimony, Martha Henderson's stern and defiant gaze was fixed on Billy Joe

Bradley, who refused to look up. To Hewey he appeared to wither physically. Bradley was a dead man and he knew it, Hewey thought.

"I have no further questions, Your Honor," said the prosecutor.

"No questions," Bradley's attorney said quickly.

"I have only one question for you, Mrs. Henderson," said Hawkins's attorney. "Did my client have any hand in this?"

"No, he did not," Martha Henderson replied. "He did not shoot at my husband, and he did not shoot at me. Throughout it all, I could hear his voice, calling loudly for them to leave me alone."

"Thank you very much, Mrs. Henderson," the attorney concluded. "I have no further questions, Your Honor."

At an unopposed request from Clay Hawkins's attorney, the judge separated the two cases and gave the Billy Joe Bradley case to the jury for deliberation. They were back in less than twenty minutes by Hewey's estimation. The jury's unanimous verdict found Bradley guilty on all counts, and the prosecutor called for the maximum sentence allowed by law.

"Mr. Bradley, you were already facing a ten-year sentence imposed by this court while you were a fugitive," the judge said. "As such, this court remands you to the custody of the state penitentiary to begin serving that sentence. . . ."

The judge paused briefly, and Hewey turned to Baker with a look of shocked disappointment.

Baker simply raised his right hand slightly, signaling patience.

". . . and at the convenience of the warden," the judge continued, "you shall be hanged by the neck until you are dead."

He emphasized that last word in what sounded to Hewey like the voice of doom, and rapped his gavel sharply. Bradley's face went white as ginned cotton, and the hair rose on the back of his neck. He buried his head in his hands.

Just as Hewey was almost beginning to entertain a twinge of sympathy, another voice rose loudly from the doorway between the courtroom and a hall. "That ain't soon enough to suit me!" said an older man. "My name's Hiram Sloan, and you led my good boy astray, started him down the road toward outlawry and got him killed. Now I'm gonna watch you die!"

The furious man reached inside his coat and drew out a revolver, pointing it in the direction of Billy Joe Bradley. The kid rose as if to make himself a better target, and Hewey could see a slight smile of relief on his face. All those at and near the defense table ducked for cover as Hiram Sloan cocked the pistol. Without giving himself time to think it over, Hewey jumped up from his seat on the center aisle, took four long strides, and placed himself squarely in front of Billy Joe Bradley.

"Don't do it, Mr. Sloan!" he implored. "Can't you see he wants you to shoot him? Billy Joe Bradley is scared to death of the hangman's noose and would rather take a bullet any day. Back off and let him sweat."

Hiram Sloan looked Hewey over closely, still holding the cocked pistol. "You! You're the one killed my boy, ain't you? I figgered on shootin' you anyway."

Hewey could see the same cold, vicious look on the older man's face that he saw in Jesse Sloan when the young outlaw thought he had Hewey helpless.

"I sure as hell don't mean to excuse Billy Joe Bradley," he said to Hiram Sloan, "but he didn't lead your boy astray. He didn't need to."

It was precisely the wrong thing to say under the circumstances, but Hewey was desperate and stalling for time. The muzzle of that pistol looked as big as one of Colonel Teddy's field cannons.

With a helpless feeling gnawing at him, Hewey couldn't tear his attention away from Sloan's gun. Then, out of the corner of his right eye, he saw a blur along the far wall. Boot heels hit the floor in rapid succession and he heard the jingle of spurs. The blur launched itself at Hiram Sloan, locked arms around the man's waist, and took him down with a solid thud. The pistol discharged harmlessly into the high ceiling, bringing down a scattering of plaster. That was when the blur resolved itself into one Speedy Martin.

Hewey's knees were beginning to quiver, and he barely made it back to his seat before they gave out completely. He turned to Baker and croaked, "I'm a damned fool."

Baker smiled broadly, placed a big, gnarled paw on Hewey's shoulder, and replied proudly, "Ya done good, Hewey. Ya done real good."

"Speedy did better" was all Hewey could say.

Baker's smile got even broader. "That boy's sure enough a caution, ain't he?"

The judge rapped his gavel twice. "This court will recess for fifteen minutes while everyone regains their composure."

Hewey was pretty sure that it would take considerably longer to regain his own composure, but it helped when he saw Chief Deputy Wiggins and two others escorting a handcuffed Hiram Sloan out the side door.

As the judge rapped his gavel again for order, Clay Hawkins's attorney rose to address the bench. "Your Honor, I wish to call my client to the stand," he said.

"You understand that this will make your client subject to questioning by the prosecution, do you not?" the judge asked.

"Yes, Your Honor, and I have advised against it, but my client wishes to speak under oath. For the record, he has given me no hint as to what he intends to say."

The prosecutor merely shrugged his shoulders.

"Very well," the judge said. "Call Clay Hawkins to the stand."

After Hawkins's swearing in, his attorney approached the witness stand.

"Mr. Hawkins, do you realize that you are testifying under a sworn oath to tell the truth?" his attorney asked.

"Yes, sir, that's the way I want it. I ain't got any reason to lie. I did what I told you I did. I was part of the express robbery and I was part of three horse stealin's. I didn't shoot nobody, though, and I didn't shoot *at* nobody."

Hawkins turned to look up at the judge.

"I'm at your mercy as far as my punishment, Judge," he said, "but before you do that, I have a little more I'd like to say under oath."

"Proceed," the judge replied.

"First off, I let greed lead me into this jackpot when Jesse and Billy Joe come to me with their plan. They told me that they'd pulled quite a few robberies and thefts before, but this was gonna be a big haul, and they needed a third man to help pull it off. Mostly they needed a third horse, but the way they figgered it, leadin' a horse would slow 'em down more than if that horse had its own rider. I don't know if they were right or wrong, but that's how they saw it. I just saw too many dollar signs to say no."

"And how did they know there would be such a load?" the judge asked.

"That's what I was leadin' up to, Judge. All along, there'd been another player in the game, somebody with fingers in a lot of pies. He told 'em who to rob and when, because he knew who'd have money and when they'd have it. He was the one put together the plan for the express robbery. I think it might have worked if them two hadn't gotten trigger-happy and killed that clerk. We all grew up together and they'd always been wild, but when I heard all them gunshots, I knew the plan had gone to hell. Pardon my language."

"Someone was guiding them, you say?" asked the judge.

"Yes, sir, somebody who kept his own hands clean, but always took a cut of what they stole. That's what they told me when they wanted my help, and I can't see how they would have known about them mine payrolls on their own."

"And did they tell you who this silent partner is?" the judge asked.

"Yes, sir, they told me it was Billy Joe's attorney, J. Pinkney Dobbs."

"And why would they do that?" the judge asked. "Why would they give away such an important secret?"

"I think they were tryin' to convince me of how foolproof the plan was," Hawkins replied. "They said they'd always been protected by one of the slickest lawyers in town, and this time would be no different, just way bigger."

The quiet murmurings of the audience suddenly rose in volume, replete with gasps and exclamations.

Hewey realized that Hawkins's story answered all the questions that had been nagging at him, and he turned to Baker, who had a sour look on his face and simply nodded his agreement before Hewey had a chance to say anything. Hewey then turned his head toward the defense table, where J. Pinkney Dobbs looked as white-faced as his client and had suddenly gone into a coughing fit.

"Mr. Hawkins," the judge continued, "that is a serious allegation, especially against an officer of this court. Do you have any evidence to back it up?"

"I don't, but I'll be willin' to guarantee that J. Pinkney Dobbs does. If you remember, the express agency manager said we took eight bags, and we only had six with us when we was caught. Jesse and Billy Joe left the other two where they said Mr. Dobbs told 'em to. That was supposed to be his share of the robbery, just like all their other thievery, and I'm bettin' them two bags are in Mr. Dobbs's safe right now."

The hubbub in the courtroom increased again, and rose in volume until the judge rapped his gavel.

"Sheriff Johnson, if you wouldn't mind escorting Mr. Dobbs to his office and surveying the contents of his safe, this court will be in recess until your return," the judge said. "Mr. Hawkins, you may step down and return to the defense table while we await the sheriff's return. Remember, you are still under oath."

Hewey watched as Sheriff Will Johnson and a deputy marched a pallid and weak-kneed J. Pinkney Dobbs from the courtroom. He turned to Baker.

"Do you reckon that sharp lawyer would be dumb enough to hang on to them bags?" he asked.

"There's no tellin'," Baker replied. "Some people get to thinkin' they're smarter than everybody else and will never get caught, and that's what gets 'em caught after all. At the very least, you know damn well he held on to the money, and it would sure be hard to justify havin' that much cash lyin' around, safe or no safe. A man would put honest money in the bank where it would earn interest."

Hewey pondered that logic, something he'd not thought of. "It makes sense," he agreed. "It's just that I never had enough money at one time to worry with a bank, so I never figgered it out that far."

"Well," said Baker, "we'll find out soon enough. Somethin' tells me Clay Hawkins wouldn't aggravate the judge with a made-up story just before bein' sentenced. That would be reckless and stupid."

"I mighta done it," Hewey admitted.

"Naw, you may be reckless, Hewey, but you ain't stupid, not by a long shot."

When the sheriff and his deputy returned with J. Pinkney Dobbs in tow, Hewey saw that the wormy-looking little lawyer was burdened by two heavy express bags, one in each hand. Despite the cool late-fall weather, Dobbs was sweating profusely, and it looked to Hewey as if a heart attack was imminent.

"Your Honor, as Mr. Dobbs here seemed so

fond of these bags," said Sheriff Will Johnson, "I thought I would let him retain possession just a little longer."

Hewey saw the same fleeting partial smile on the judge's face that he'd seen earlier. The stern look quickly returned, and he thought it looked especially cold as the judge addressed Dobbs.

"J. Pinkney Dobbs," the judge said, "you are an acute embarrassment to this court. I await the prosecution's charges against you, and in the meantime I remand you to the sheriff's care pending trial. Sheriff, Mr. Dobbs is all yours, and there will be no bail. If anyone arrives at your office claiming to have a bail order, you have this court's permission to shoot him."

Sheriff Johnson chuckled at that, and Dobbs briefly looked as if he might protest, but that ended as soon as he got a look at the judge's scowl.

As Sheriff Johnson led Dobbs from the courtroom, the judge rapped his gavel again, restored a semblance of silence, and turned to Clay Hawkins. "Please rise, Mr. Hawkins," he said.

With Hawkins and his attorney both standing, the judge pronounced sentence.

"Mr. Hawkins," he said evenly, "the crimes you have admitted to in this court would ordinarily lead me to impose a sentence of ten to twelve years in the penitentiary. In light of your voluntary admission of guilt, however, and in recognition of your invaluable help in ridding this region of J. Pinkney Dobbs, I have selected a sentence of five to six years.

With good behavior, it might even be less. Do you have anything to say to this court?"

"Yes, sir. Since I'm still under oath, I'd like to say I'm sorry for what I've done and swear that I'll never do anything like it again. And I want to thank you, Judge, for giving me a break."

"I am remanding you to the La Plata County Sheriff's Office to begin serving your sentence. I expect your testimony when this court tries J. Pinkney Dobbs, and you will remain in local custody until that time."

He rapped his gavel again. "This court stands adjourned."

CHAPTER ELEVEN

Hewey and Baker exited through the side door after watching the courtroom spectators ball up at the big rear double doors like a herd of cattle all bunched at a gateway. Those who wanted out were threading themselves through a crowd of others chattering and blocking their way.

"Have you noticed how different this crowd is than the ones at the first trial?" Hewey said to Baker.

"They look like pretty much the same people to me," Baker answered.

"I'm talkin' about the attitude," Hewey replied. "After the first trial, people were stiff-jawed and serious-actin'. These folks are grinnin' and visitin' around like they just left the big tent at a travelin' circus. That seems sorta odd, given the serious nature of the thing."

Baker pondered that briefly before answering. "I think that's what my old daddy called 'whistlin' past the graveyard.' They've heard some awful things this time around, and they all realize that it could have happened to any of 'em. They're just damned lucky it didn't, and they're tryin' to convince themselves that it never will."

"That makes sense," Hewey said. "Nobody wants to think that such meanness can still happen in this modern, civilized age, I guess."

"No matter how many fancy gadgets people think up, human nature don't change," Baker pointed out. "There'll always be bad ones amongst us, and it's hard to pretend it away when it's right there starin' you in the face. So folks laugh and make out like they don't have goose bumps."

"You've tracked down some sure-enough bad ol' boys, and I've climbed on horses that'd give any sane man goose bumps," Hewey replied in agreement. "We're just lucky that we've both got a touch of crazy in us."

"Well, ain't we the philosophers," Baker said in amusement. "The cook ought to have dinner ready directly. Let's go down to the wagon and maybe be first in line."

"Yeah, I philosophize better on a full belly," Hewey said.

⬥

When they reached the wagon, Hewey found that some of the Slash M hands had been at the trial and others hung around camp nursing queasy stomachs and ringing heads, symptoms he recognized from repeated experience. As best he could figure out, the two groups were the same on both days of the proceedings. As a result, the trial spectators were busy telling the others what they'd seen and heard.

Hewey was an immediate celebrity upon arrival.

"Damn, Hewey," said a cowboy Hewey knew only as Charlie, "steppin' in front of Billy Joe Bradley took guts!" The rest of the crew seemed to agree.

"What it took was a brass-plated idiot," Hewey replied, drawing laughter from the entire assembly.

"Why did you do it?" asked a hand named Henry.

"It was just as I told Hiram Sloan," Hewey answered. "Billy Joe Bradley is scared half to death of hangin', and ol' Sloan was about to let him off easy with a bullet."

"I guess you'll get a front-row seat when they drop the trapdoor out from under him," offered a voice from behind him.

"No," Hewey said, "I've been to one hangin', and that was enough for me. I want to know when it's been done, but I just don't have the stomach for it, not even for Billy Joe Bradley."

That seemed to surprise most of the hands, though a couple murmured in agreement. Hanley Baker stepped in at that point.

"I'm with Hewey," he said. "I've seen several hangin's too many, and I know the SOBs deserved it, because I tracked 'em down. I'll be happy to know that nobody has Billy Joe Bradley to worry about anymore, but I'll let somebody else watch."

"I'll tell you who was the real hero in that courtroom, and that's Speedy," Hewey told the group. "That boy saved me from a bad case of lead poisonin'. Where the hell is he, anyway?"

"Trace buttonholed him right outside the courtroom and offered to buy him a drink. You don't see the foreman do that very often." It was Henry again.

Hewey and Baker both grinned at that.

"I hope he buys him two," Baker said.

The next day, Hewey had just finished his noon meal when he heard someone calling his name.

"Mr. Baker! Mr. Calloway!"

Hewey looked up from the washtub of hot, soapy water where he'd just added his tin plate. It was the express office agent, Ben Phillips.

"What can we do for you, Mr. Phillips?" Baker still held his plate but had nearly mopped it clean with his third biscuit. He dropped the half-eaten biscuit onto the plate, wiped his right hand on his britches, and extended it to shake.

Hewey stepped forward to do the same, and Phillips shook each man's hand vigorously. "It's not what you can do for me," he said, "it's what I can do for you. My bosses back East have authorized me to provide the two of you with a reward for capturing those outlaws and returning the mine payrolls."

"Mr. Phillips, we didn't expect any reward," Baker said. "Those three needed to be brought to justice for what else they'd done, too. When we set out, we weren't even sure we were trackin' the same outlaws."

Hewey nodded agreement.

"Well, gentlemen," Phillips said, "I can't make you take the five hundred dollars, but I surely wish you would."

"Just curious," Baker said, "but why didn't we hear about a reward earlier, when it might have put a lot of bloodhounds on the trail? That's the way rewards usually work."

"I asked the same question, Mr. Baker," Phillips replied. "I was told that the company preferred not to publicize the loss of so much money for fear that it might cost us customers. I told them that cat was already out of the bag, but they held firm to their position."

"Just when you think you've heard it all . . ." Baker said with a shake of his head.

Hewey took a step back. "I've never seen that much money at one time except once on a poker table," he replied, "and I didn't win it. In fact, my last six bits was in the pile. To tell you the truth, I've already got more money in my pocket than I know what to do with. If I had another two hunnerd and fifty bucks, I'd just waste it on foolishness.

"But I've got an idea where it would do some good. Did your clerk leave a family?"

"A widow, Mr. Calloway, but the company has already dealt with that," Phillips answered.

"Well then," Hewey continued, "I have another idea. I'd appreciate it if you'd give my half to the Henderson couple. You probably saw them in the courtroom."

Before Phillips could say anything, Baker spoke up. "That's a damn good notion, Hewey. They can have my half, too. Those good people have been through a lot, and a young couple like that, just startin' out and havin' such a setback, it might be a real comfort to 'em. Hewey, sometimes you still surprise me."

"You gentlemen seem to be set on that, so the Henderson couple it is," Phillips said with a smile. "I was already feeling good about this little chore, and the two of you have made it even better. But Durango is a big place. Do you have any idea where I might find the Hendersons?"

"I do," said a voice Hewey recognized immediately as Bryce McKenzie's. "I overheard enough walking up here to get the gist. The Hendersons are at my hotel, guests of the Slash M. It was just a gesture, nothing like what you men are offering. If you will come with me, Mr. Phillips, I'll take you to their room."

After McKenzie and Phillips left, Baker turned to Hewey. "What say you and me go hunt up Rutherford and ol' Speedy? I'll stand you to a whisky."

"If it's all the same to you, I think I'll stick to beer," Hewey replied. "I don't know what's come over me, but whisky just doesn't sound all that good right now."

"I reckon you're gettin' old," Baker joshed. "Happens to ever'body eventually."

Hewey responded with a scowl, but he had a nagging feeling that Baker might be right.

They found Rutherford and Speedy at the saloon nearest the campsite, the same establishment the Slash M hands had frequented over the previous two nights. A few of the other hands were already there, but Rutherford and Speedy sat at a table apart. Rutherford was slowly nursing a beer, and Speedy had a whisky glass. Rutherford motioned for the latecomers to join them. Speedy looked a little unsteady.

They had barely sat down when Speedy stood up. "Mr. Rutherford," he said, "I really appreciate those two drinks, but I'm not all that used to whisky. I think I'd best go back to camp and turn in. It's been a long day."

Hewey stood back up to shake Speedy's hand. "You saved my bacon back yonder in the courtroom," he told the tipsy youngster. "I'd sure hoped to buy you a drink or two."

"Thank you, Mr. Calloway," Speedy replied, "but Mr. Rutherford's already done that, and I think I've had enough."

"We'll do it another time, then," Hewey told him.

"Yes, sir," Speedy said. "I'd like that. I think." He turned and walked slowly toward the door, giving wide roundance to the tables and chairs he encountered on his way.

"That Speedy is a good kid," Rutherford said. "I hope we can keep him around for a long time and he doesn't drift away like so many cowboys do."

"Something tells me he'll stick," Baker said. "Just a feelin', but he seems to have that in him."

"And how about you boys?" Rutherford asked. "Are you going to stick for the winter?"

"I've got no place I'd rather be this late in the year," Hewey answered.

"It's temptin'," Baker replied, "but I have a cabin northeast of here that I haven't seen in a while. I think I'll hole up there for the winter. Just need to provision a little and chop some firewood. Deer will feed me, maybe even an elk."

"Hewey, they tell me you favor line-camp work in the winter," Rutherford said. "I have a camp job if you're interested. The usual thing, looking for stock stranded in drifts, throwing adventurous ones back toward lower country."

"I've spent quite a few winters like that, and it suits me," Hewey answered by way of acceptance. "I get a little tired of talkin' to my horse before it's all done, but otherwise I do fine."

"Well, you won't have to talk to your horse this time around, because we always insist on two men in a camp. There's a hundred ways a man can get in serious trouble up there, and I don't like to find dead bodies when the snow melts. Any idea who you'd like siding you?"

Hewey thought for a few seconds. "If he'll go, I'd sure take Speedy." It brought that crooked grin to his face. "The kid doesn't have much quit in him."

"We'll ask him in the morning," Rutherford said, "but I've got a hunch he'll be tickled."

"Does the Slash M supply snowshoes?" Baker asked mischievously.

"Why would I need snowshoes?" Hewey said. "I've never needed 'em before."

"You've never wintered in Colorado," Baker replied, trying to keep a straight face. "The snowshoes are for when the snow's too deep for a horse."

They all three laughed at that, but then Hewey turned to Rutherford. "He ain't serious, is he?"

Hewey, Baker, and Trace Rutherford were finishing breakfast the next morning, Baker and Rutherford sitting on their bedrolls and Hewey squatting on his haunches; he was an early riser and his bedroll was already in the wagon. Rutherford spotted Speedy pitching his bedroll into the rapidly filling wagon and called out to him. "Speedy! Got a minute?"

"Yes, sir, Mr. Rutherford! I'll be right there!" Speedy answered, prompting Rutherford to shake his head.

"I still have a ways to go before I get him to drop the 'sir,'" he said to Hewey and Baker.

"Good manners is usually easy to break," Hewey observed with his typical crooked grin. "That boy's mama sure branded 'em deep into his hide, but I'll bet I can corrupt it out of him after a few months."

When Speedy arrived, Rutherford asked how he would like a camp job. "Hewey has offered to spend the winter at the Robinson camp, and he needs a partner."

"Really?" Speedy answered. "I'd sure like that, Mr. Calloway."

"Good, but if I can't get you to call me Hewey, the deal's off," Hewey told him with both eyes squinting in an expression that he hoped looked serious and a little sinister.

"Yes, sir, Mr. Callo—Hewey."

"And you'd best pack on all the weight you can before we go," Hewey warned, "because my cookin' is just barely tolerable at best."

"Oh, don't worry about that, Mr. Ca—Hewey. I cook pretty good."

"You don't say," Hewey replied. "Where'd you learn to cook?"

"My mama taught me when I was a kid," Speedy answered. "She was a good cook, and I picked up a lot of it. Her biscuits were the best I've ever tasted, and mine are pretty good if I do say so myself."

Hewey's eyes lit up. "This is shapin' up to be a dandy winter, even if I have to learn to walk in snowshoes."

"There's snowshoes?" Speedy asked with a puzzled expression.

Baker and Rutherford both stifled laughs.

As the cook began breaking camp, Hewey noticed that he had a helper. "I ain't never seen that youngster before," he told Rutherford.

"He's the new kid wrangler," Rutherford replied, "fresh off a Kansas farm and green as spring corn, but I liked something about him, so he's the one I picked. He'll be doing a lot of odd jobs until we take a remuda out, but that's how they all get started."

"You sure hit the jackpot when you picked Speedy," Hewey said. "Let's hope your picker's still workin' that good."

"I always hold my breath a little," Rutherford conceded.

Over Rutherford's shoulder Hewey saw two familiar figures approaching, one with his arm around the other. "Baker!" he hollered. "I think we have company comin'."

Baker looked up from where he was double-checking the ropes around his bedroll, smiled broadly, and joined Hewey.

"Mr. Calloway, Mr. Baker, I don't know how Nate and I could possibly accept such a generous gift," said Martha Henderson. "The two of you risked your lives for that reward, and to give it to us . . ." Her voice trailed off and she appeared ready to cry.

"We'll make it easy to accept," Hewey replied with a serious demeanor few ever saw in him, "because there ain't no way we'll take it back."

"Besides," Baker joined in, "we had no idea there would be a reward. We done what we done because it needed doin', and we'd both do it again if come to that."

"Now, I don't think I'd go quite that far," Hewey said. "The first time I was ignorant. I know better now." Hewey had shed the serious look and reverted to his usual crooked grin.

The Hendersons both laughed, and Baker pretended surprise at Hewey's reluctance.

"I have a brother back in Texas," Hewey continued. "He's married and has a family, but they're doin' okay. If he and my sister-in-law had faced the same setback you folks did when they were startin' out, I can't imagine where they'd be today.

"I wouldn't do anything but squander money like that anyway, and I know Baker would do the same—"

"It'd just take me a lot longer," Baker interjected.

"—so it only made sense to pass it on to folks who could make good, honest use of it," Hewey concluded. "Consider the subject closed."

Nate Henderson reached out to shake hands, pumping both men's arms vigorously in turn.

Martha Henderson's eyes welled with tears, and she startled Hewey by giving him a sudden hug and a kiss on the cheek. He took a step back when she released him, and his eyes went wide. Baker had a couple of seconds' warning before she threw her arms around him and planted a kiss on his cheek as well, but he was still as stunned as Hewey.

It was then the Hendersons' turn to laugh, Martha wiping away tears with the bottom of her apron.

"Baker, we need to do this sort of thing more often," Hewey quipped.

As the couple turned to leave, Nate Henderson stopped. "I sure hope we see both of you again," he said.

"If I'm ever within fifty miles, I'll make it a point to stop by," Hewey said.

"You have my word," Baker added.

It was still early in the day when Hewey saw the Hendersons pull out of the wagonyard and turn left onto the street. The Slash M cook and his new young helper were still a little short of finishing up, but that meant the entire cowboy crew wouldn't be far behind the Hendersons all the way, should they have difficulties.

Artie Samuels and the Swensons hadn't left yet, and Hewey could see them less than a hundred yards away. He wanted to say his goodbyes to them before they left, but he would never have thought of making such a trip afoot, so he was saddling his horse. Trace Rutherford had done the same, and he fell in beside Hewey as they rode up the alley. They encountered Samuels on horseback and the Swensons in their buckboard, visiting as if they were nearby neighbors.

Hewey tipped his hat to Maria Swenson, and before he could open his mouth, Rutherford extended an invitation to all of them to stay at the Slash M headquarters that evening. It was typical cow country courtesy, but the same unwritten code frowned on those who would presume such an invitation without receiving it.

"I appreciate the invite," said Artie Samuels. "It'll be a lot more pleasant to spend the evening around civilized folks than to spread my roll somewhere alongside the road."

"Maria and I will also be pleased to accept," said Lars Swenson, and his wife smiled and nodded her head.

"None of you will need to worry about cooking your own supper," Rutherford added. "You can take your meals at the bunkhouse table. Our cook's a good one, and not as cranky as some. He may even show off with something special for company."

"I sure wish you'd managed to catch the Hendersons, too," Hewey said.

"Didn't have to," Rutherford replied. "I invited them earlier while you and Baker were grinning yourselves silly over Mrs. Henderson's show of affection."

"How come I didn't see you?" Hewey asked.

"I expect you couldn't see anything for all those stars in your eyes."

Samuels and the Swensons looked confused. "It's

a long story," Rutherford said, grinning, "but I'm sure it will make the rounds before nightfall."

"I'd tell you myself," Hewey added, "if I wasn't the shy and bashful sort. Anyway, I come up here to say goodbye, but it looks like I'm a mornin' too early. See you folks this evenin'."

Hewey and Rutherford rode the short distance back to the camp. The coffeepot still sat over the last embers from the fire, and Rutherford took two cups from the still-open chuckbox.

"Better make that three cups," Hewey said. "Baker's on his way back here." The former lawman had caught, saddled, and ridden his horse the short distance from the nearest large corral, where the Slash M mounts had been turned out. He dismounted and tied his reins to the big rear wheel of the wagon before crossing to the firepit. Hewey thought his limp looked more pronounced.

"That leg bothering you this mornin'?" he asked.

Baker took a cup from Rutherford, poured it half full of coffee, then answered, "There's a change comin' in the weather. A big one unless my ol' leg is lyin' to me. This time of year I never want to doubt it, 'cause a man can sure get into trouble if he ain't careful."

"Are you certain you want to try making it to your cabin right now?" Rutherford asked. "You're welcome to come back to the ranch and try again later."

"Appreciate the offer," Baker said. "I do sure enough, but there's places I can hole up between here and there if need be. The best spot is a little better than halfway, an old cabin built stout like mine. Belonged to some people who passed on several years ago. At the least it'll turn the wind, and I can have a fire to take the chill off."

"Well, if you change your mind, we'll keep the welcome mat out," Rutherford replied. It didn't sound to Hewey as though Rutherford was any better at changing Baker's mind than Hewey had ever been.

"I drew you a map to my cabin," Baker said to Hewey as he handed over a scrap of paper. "It's crude, but you can foller it."

They all three perked up as they heard the rattle and jingle of harnessed mules coming down the alley.

"We'd best get clean out of Cookie's way," Hewey said. "It don't pay to rile a man of his perfession."

They gulped the last sips of their coffee, rinsed them under a spigot on the water barrel, and Rutherford put them back into their cubbyhole in the chuckbox. Baker untied his horse and led him near the tree where Hewey and Rutherford had tied up, well out of the way. It took only a few minutes for the cook and his helper to hitch the team; every farm boy knew how to harness and hitch a brace of mules.

The wagon was quickly on the move, and the Slash M hands filed in behind it as it passed by them in the alley. Hewey, Baker, and Rutherford brought up the rear. As the processional reached the street and turned left, the trailing trio reined up. Trace Rutherford reached over to shake hands with Baker. "You know you're always welcome," he said before spurring his horse into a slow lope to catch up with the hands.

"I sure have enjoyed these last few months," Hewey said. "Well, some of it anyway. You take care of yourself."

"Aw, don't go gettin' mushy on me," Baker said with a chuckle before reining his horse to the right. A few yards down the street he twisted in the saddle and yelled back to Hewey, "Come hunt me up in the spring, why don't ya!"

AUTHOR'S NOTE

During my younger days, I spent as much time as possible on the McElroy Ranch in West Texas's Crane and Upton counties. Managed by my grandfather Buck Kelton, the McElroy was where my father, Elmer Kelton, and my uncles grew up. The sprawling two-hundred-section operation still retained much of the old way of doing things, providing a taste of the Old West, at least in the eyes of a youngster. Horses were still essential for cattle work, and no one thought twice about having us mounted alongside the grown men, or sending us to flush cattle out of brushy draws. It was just how things had always been done, and it was a grand way to grow up; one available to too few young people, even then. Decades later, when I was running my own cattle with my own money on the line, I better appreciated some of my grandfather's habits, like picking up rusty nuts, bolts, and hinges.

Granddad also taught me other things that I wasn't even aware I was learning, things that would serve me well in later life. Until I completed *The Unlikely Lawman* it didn't dawn on me that I had modeled Hanley Baker in part on Granddad, particularly his habit of "volunteering" Hewey Calloway to do things Hewey didn't necessarily want to do, compounded by his aversion to explaining what sort of project he and Hewey were undertaking.

"Come on, let's go," Granddad would say as he drove up to me in the pickup. It wasn't an invitation but an order. I got in and off we went. I naturally wanted to know what we were about to do, but I soon learned that Granddad didn't like questions, so I began trying to puzzle it out for myself. If the black steel toolbox was in the bed of the truck, we were going to work on a windmill; if instead it was a square-bladed shovel and a worn-out broom, I would have the pleasure of cleaning several inches of stinking black muck out of a large water trough, et cetera. I was doing what the cowboys called "reading sign," and didn't realize it.

A typical Granddad story involved a wrench. Granddad was working on a water trough in the headquarters' corrals and I was his pint-sized "gofer."

"Run get me a Stillson," he said.

I assumed a Stillson was a wrench, but that's as close as I could come. Nevertheless, I ran to the toolhouse about a hundred yards away, grabbed a wrench, and ran back.

"Naw," Granddad said, employing several expletives in the process. "Get me a Stillson!"

Another trip and another wrong wrench. I think I made three failed efforts. Granddad was getting frustrated and I was both frustrated and winded. Finally, I grabbed one of the remaining wrenches and trotted back.

Lucky guess.

"Yeah, that's the Stillson. Why didn't you bring that one the first damned time?"

It was one of the most common pipe wrenches, and evidently the Stillson company introduced it in Granddad's younger days, so it would always be a Stillson to him, no matter what name was cast into the handle. After that experience, it's always been a Stillson to me, as well.

One of the toughest puzzles I had to solve was classic Granddad. He took me with him one late afternoon, and we drove to a set of corrals where we did nothing but make sure the gates were swinging, then went home. The next morning, I woke up to the sound of pickups and horse trailers driving away—I'd been left behind. My grandmother was much more open to questions, and I discovered that I was expected to take the cattle truck to the corrals where we had been the previous evening, an ambitious chore for a boy just out of the second grade and still too small to reach the pedals and see over the dashboard at the same time. Worse, I hadn't been paying close attention to our route the evening before, so I was navigating by guesswork.

I found the right pasture, then turned off the main road onto a series of branching two-rut pickup trails. Every time a trail branched off I would stop the truck and look for our tire tracks from the previous evening. I finally found the corrals, and learned another object lesson—pay attention even when it doesn't seem important.

If I had followed that lesson, of course, I would have recognized Granddad's contribution to Hanley Baker before I finished the book.

All in all, it reinforces Dad's observation that if characters come to life they will take a book in directions the author never intended, and if they don't, he won't have a book anyway. Dad brought Hewey Calloway to life, and Hanley Baker developed before my eyes. I wrote *The Unlikely Lawman* based on where Dad said he wanted it to begin and how he wanted to launch it; from there I had no idea what his plot would be because he never wrote an outline or synopsis for a book, preferring to let his characters drive the plot. That's what I've done as well. I also knew where he wanted it to end, and this book stops well short of there. The follow-up book will end as Dad intended, however, come hell or high water.

Steve Kelton
May 9, 2021

ACKNOWLEDGMENTS

I thank my dad, Elmer Kelton, who created Hewey Calloway, and my wife, Karen McGinnis, who kept asking if Hewey was talking to me.

Forge

Award-winning authors
Compelling stories

. . . .

Please join us at the website
below for more information
about this author and other great
Forge selections, and to sign up for
our monthly newsletter!

. . . . www.tor-forge.com . . . .